TELL ME SOMETHING . . .

"Look," I said, "you better leave. I want to unpack by my-self." And, as she continued to kneel there on the floor, I walked to the open door and stood by it.

She waited just past the point at which I was sure she wasn't going to move. Then she got up, elaborately dusting off her knees. "Tell me something," she said, as if casually. "How did you feel when she went down?"

All the air left the room.

Lily was leaning forward, her gaze avid, sucking at mine. "Tell me. Did you feel . . . *powerful*? Were you glad? Even . . . for just a minute?"

I had words, somewhere inside me, but for a long moment they were formless. I thought, *She's just a kid, she's just a kid*, but that didn't help. Greg and Emily and I had been kids, too. Being under eighteen didn't mean you were innocent. Or harmless.

BOOKS BY NANCY WERLIN

THE KILLER'S COUSIN

NANCY WERLIN

speak

An Imprint of Penguin Group (USA) Inc.

For my parents,
Elaine and Arnold Werlin,
with love and gratitude

SPEAK
Published by the Penguin Group
Penguin Group (USA) Inc., 345 Hudson Street, New York, New York 10014, U.S.A.
Penguin Group (Canada), 90 Eglinton Avenue East, Suite 700, Toronto, Ontario, Canada M4P 2Y3
(a division of Pearson Penguin Canada Inc.)
Penguin Books Ltd, 80 Strand, London WC2R 0RL, England
Penguin Ireland, 25 St Stephen's Green, Dublin 2, Ireland (a division of Penguin Books Ltd)
Penguin Group (Australia), 250 Camberwell Road, Camberwell, Victoria 3124, Australia
(a division of Pearson Australia Group Pty Ltd)
Penguin Books India Pvt Ltd, 11 Community Centre, Panchsheel Park, New Delhi - 110 017, India
Penguin Group (NZ), 67 Apollo Drive, Rosedale, North Shore 0632, New Zealand
(a division of Pearson New Zealand Ltd)
Penguin Books (South Africa) (Pty) Ltd, 24 Sturdee Avenue, Rosebank, Johannesburg 2196, South Africa

Penguin Books Ltd, Registered Offices: 80 Strand, London WC2R 0RL, England

First published in the United States of America by Delacorte Press, 1998
Published by Speak, an imprint of Penguin Group (USA) Inc., 2009

5 7 9 10 8 6

Copyright © Nancy Werlin, 1998
All rights reserved

THE LIBRARY OF CONGRESS HAS CATALOGED THE DELACORTE EDITION AS FOLLOWS:
Werlin, Nancy.
The killer's cousin / Nancy Werlin.
p. cm.
Summary: After being acquitted of murder, seventeen-year-old David goes to stay
with relatives in Cambridge, Massachusetts, where he finds himself forced to face his past
as he learns more about his strange young cousin Lily.
ISBN: 0-385-32560-6 (hc)
[1. Emotional problems—Fiction. 2. Cousins—Fiction. 3. Guilt—Fiction.
4. Murder—Fiction. 5. Family problems—Fiction.] I. Title.
PZ7.W4713Ki 1998
[Fic]—dc21
98012950 CIP AC

Speak ISBN 978-0-14-241373-9

Printed in the United States of America

PROLOGUE

My name, David Bernard Yaffe, will sound familiar, but you won't remember why—at least not at first. Most people, I've found, do not. I'm grateful for that. It gives me some space, however brief. However certain eventually to disintegrate.

When you do remember, it won't be my face you recall. Not that the press didn't shoot plenty of pictures. But it's the photograph of my parents that was famous. That's the one that's developing now in your mind's eye, behind your concentrated frown.

A regular-looking couple in their early fifties. The man thick-haired, blue-eyed. Groomed. The woman's emotions shielded by dark glasses, but her hands betraying her as they clutch the man's coat sleeve, biting through to the arm beneath. His other hand is over hers, comforting—but the man's attention is clearly elsewhere, ahead. Behind them, you can just see the

1

bleak facade of the courthouse in Baltimore on a bitterly cold day.

The man is looking directly into the camera. I can read his expression, but I defy you to do so. He is practiced at concealing his thoughts, my father. He's a lawyer. A *criminal* lawyer. You'll remember that now, too. Some of the tabloids said it was why I got off. *Behind-scenes wheeling and dealing?* they asked. *Powerful litigator calls in favors?* they hinted.

You'd like to know, I'm sure. Everyone would like to know. But I won't lead you on. This—the story I have to tell—is not about me and it is not about that. I won't deceive you about it, because I am at this moment no more willing to talk about Emily and what happened my senior year of high school—my first senior year—than I ever was.

No, this is about my second senior year. About Lily. Lily, cousin of a killer. My Massachusetts cousin. Lily. I need to talk about Lily.

CHAPTER 1

My cousin Lily was eleven years old when I moved into the third floor of my uncle Vic and aunt Julia's triple-decker house at the northern end of Cambridge, Massachusetts. I drove to Cambridge from Baltimore, dully, doggedly, through one long day in sticky late-August heat the summer . . . the summer after. My car had air-conditioning, but I kept the windows down and let the fierce hot wind off Interstate 95 slam me in the face and chest. I couldn't be bothered to switch CDs, and so I listened over and over to R.E.M. doing the firehouse song—the only one on the album that really penetrated.

I was almost eighteen, but instead of packing for college, I was headed for a private prep school where I would repeat my senior year of high school. I needed to do it, needed to finish and finish well, if I was to have any chance of getting into what my father called a "decent college." If I was to get my life "back on track."

"As if I were a train," I'd said to them.

"You'll care later," my mother said. "Davey . . ." She faltered over my old nickname and then went on. "David, I swear it. I promise."

What could I say to that? I had no better ideas. Just revulsion. Just general, all-purpose, constant nausea.

I knew I should be grateful that Vic and Julia had agreed to take me. Grateful for shelter far from Baltimore; grateful to be away from the Baltimore and D.C. press. From my ex-friends. From my parents. Grateful to have a future at all. Grateful, grateful, grateful. I knew what I was supposed to feel.

"Vic and Julia and Lily are your family," my mother said, urgent to persuade me. "Families stick together in . . ." She hesitated, as always. "In crises. Let them help you, David. Let them help us. Please."

In a way it was hilarious, hearing my mother sing the praises of her brother, Vic Shaughnessy, and his wife, Julia. Because the fact was, our family hadn't had much to do with theirs, and it wasn't because Maryland to Massachusetts was too far to travel. We stayed distant from my mother's family because, in my childhood, my mother and her sister-in-law were engaged in ongoing guerrilla warfare.

"Well, look," my mother would say, ripping open a thick cream envelope in mid-December. "Julia's gone all out on the Christmas cards this year. A Botticelli Madonna! Religious, but so tasteful!" And she would fire back an envelope containing a construction-paper menorah (commissioned from me) plus the contents of

4

half a tube of silver glitter. "Imagine it, Stuart," she'd say to my father triumphantly. "Glitter all over Julia's clean floor."

"Eileen," my father would say, his eyes amused, "is this necessary?"

"Absolutely."

It was no secret that Julia disapproved of my parents' marriage and of our Judaism. Of my mother's in-your-face conversion from Catholicism. And, in those innocent days, my mother positively enjoyed disliking Julia. "Behave yourself," she would threaten me, "or I'll pack you off to Cambridge to live with your aunt Julia and go to Catholic school with your cousin Kathy!" At that time, Lily, twelve years younger than her sister, Kathy, had not yet started school.

Odd that all these years later, my mother really had packed me off to Massachusetts to live with Vic and Julia, and to enroll in the same Catholic prep school that Kathy had attended.

I remembered Kathy vividly, though we'd met only once, when Lily was born. I'd been seven, and fascinated with my pretty older cousin. I loved Kathy's red hair; her laugh. I followed her everywhere that week she stayed with us, and she let me. She spent her own money at the corner store to buy me ice cream.

She had been dead four years now, Kathy.

"Stuart, they understand something of what we're feeling," my mother had said to my father, after Vic called and made the offer. I wasn't meant to overhear. "Because of Kathy," my mother said. "Because of Kathy, my brother understands."

* * *

5

The words *back on track, back on track* took up a measured beat in my head as I went through Central Square and, following Vic's directions, got myself on Massachusetts Avenue and nosed north.

At the umpteenth light I spotted the sign for Walden Street. I signaled for a left-hand turn, waited for the light to turn yellow and narrowly avoided colliding with an oncoming car whose driver audibly swore at me. My stomach clenched; I was too shocked even to swear back. And in that flash of danger—the few seconds when the Cambridge driver ignored traffic laws and barreled straight into my right-of-way—I suddenly knew something. I didn't want to die.

Other cars were honking furiously at me. I opened my eyes. Gently, I pressed on the gas again and pulled onto Walden, and then, a few streets later, onto Vic and Julia's street.

Like its neighbors, Hubbardston Street in North Cambridge was one-way and narrow, packed with tall wood frame houses, and full of screaming kids on Rollerblades playing street hockey. Confused by the kids and by the way each house had multiple numbers, I drove past No. 87 and had to go around the block again. This time I found Vic and Julia's driveway. I backed into it with difficulty, turned off the car's motor, and looked out at the house.

And met the green eyes of a prepubescent girl who was sitting alone on the front steps, hugging her bare knees. Lily.

I took a deep breath. There was no choice; I got out of the car. Stretched my cramped shoulder and leg muscles; felt the bones crackle. "Hey, Lily," I croaked. I

hadn't spoken since ordering at the drive-through Mc-
Donald's in New Jersey at noon. I cleared my throat.
"How are you?"

She didn't move. She was small, pasty-faced, and
slightly chubby, with thick shaggy brown hair almost
hiding her eyes. Her chin stuck out; her elbows defended her body. I had a sudden memory of the last
time I'd seen her, on a chair at the funeral home, her
feet dangling. Old and middle-aged people filling the
room, crowding around the closed coffin, around Vic
and Julia. No friends of Kathy's. No kids at all, except
Lily. And me.

I had been having trouble breathing in the stuffy funeral home. I'd kept staring at the polished mahogany
coffin lid, imagining Kathy beneath it; recalling horror
movies I'd seen in which people were buried alive.

I had wanted, powerfully, to get out of there. I had
certainly not thought to spend any time with Lily. Lily,
who had stared at everything from her chair. Who got
paler and paler as the day of the funeral wore on, but
who did not cry, even during the eulogy.

But that was then. I drew a breath. Awkwardly, I
approached Lily and sat down beside her on the steps.
"It was a long drive," I said.

Her arms tightened around her knees. She looked
steadily at me. It was difficult to look back at her, but I
had learned how to meet people's gazes, and I did it.

"Hi," she said grudgingly. One last, long stare, and
then she got up. "I'll tell them you're here." Before I
could move, the screen door slammed behind her as
she pounded up the inside stairs to the second floor.

I got up from the stoop, not knowing if I should fol-

7

low Lily, and waited, shifting from foot to foot. The noise from the street hockey paused for a split second before exploding into an uproar of excitement as one kid—ten million years younger than me—made a spectacular goal. In that instant of silence, somewhere above my head I heard a woman say, "Tell your father, not me." Julia?

But before I had time to think anything, Vic came bursting out of the front door and without warning enveloped me in an enormous hug. "David! I was starting to get worried—come in!"

He released me, but I could still feel the shocking imprint of his arms. I backed up a half step. When was the last time my father had touched me?

We went upstairs, Vic exploding with words as if he hadn't talked to anyone for a month. ". . . We rent the first floor to a girl, a college student. She's an artist but always pays the rent on time. We live on the second . . . You'll want something to drink? . . . You should call Eileen and Stuart to tell them you arrived safely . . . You're sure you're not hungry? . . . You'll be on the third floor; I'll show you after you've had a chance to relax . . . Sit down, sit down . . . ." He forced me into a kitchen chair and bustled around, getting a Coke for me and a lemonade for Lily, who had perched on the edge of the counter and was watching my every move.

Vic had put on weight in the four years since I'd seen him. He'd been gaunt then, unhealthy, but the new weight wasn't right either. His flesh hung from his cheeks like a basset hound's, and his eyes were anxious

8

and tired. I accepted the Coke. I looked around for Julia.

"You'll be very comfortable, David," Vic was saying. "It's really a little apartment, not a spare bedroom. But we can't rent it because it has only one entrance, and fire codes require two. Plus, the entrance is through our apartment, so, well, we wouldn't be comfortable with just anyone. But you're family, of course."

He sounded somehow uneasy. More so, even, than I had expected. Or maybe I thought that because I caught Lily's face just then, squinched up in scorn. And because there was no sign of Julia. But I followed Vic's lead.

"It's a big help," I said. "Your having me." I paused and then said it. "Thank you." I looked right into his eyes, as my mother would want me to do. "Thank you, Uncle Vic."

"Well," said Vic. His shoulders moved awkwardly, but he did look straight back at me. "Well . . ."

The pause lengthened. I finished my drink, put down the can, and said, "Could I have a look at my room . . . at the apartment now?"

"Sure," said Vic. He took me on a tour, Lily trailing behind.

Vic and Julia's second-floor apartment followed a plan that I later learned was standard in Cambridge multifamily houses. Stairs from the ground floor ended in a hallway that ran the length of the house. On one side of the hall were a bath and two bedrooms. On the other sat the kitchen, a dining room, and at the front of the house, the living room.

In the living room, Vic unlocked and pulled open a door that I would have guessed concealed a closet. "Up here," he said. Behind him, I saw a narrow wooden staircase. It climbed steeply upward between walls of frayed and darkened yellow wallpaper. At the top was another door.

They were putting me in the attic.

"One day, I'll need to rebuild these stairs," Vic said as we climbed. Silently, I agreed; I could hear the creak, feel the give, of the old wood under me. Lily crowded me closely from behind. For a moment we all stood on the narrow steps in the dark. Then Vic opened the door to the attic, and sunlight burst in around us.

A living room and bedroom lay snugly under the eaves, with a counter separating a modern kitchenette from the living room. The furniture was spare but sufficient—bed and nightstand, small sofa, table and chairs. Fresh white paint dressed the walls; the wooden floor gleamed with polish. The bathroom was compact but complete, its one flaw the tininess of the tub. But who cared? I took showers anyway.

"Wow," I said to Vic. "It's a great place."

"I just installed the kitchenette a couple of years ago," Vic said, "and put the skylights in the roof. Divided the space." He smiled shyly at me. "It used to be just one big room, with a bathroom that I added when . . ." He stopped and bit his lip.

"It's great," I said again, sincerely. "I'm—"

"I should live here," said Lily. She had seated herself cross-legged in the very center of the living room floor. Her face was expressionless. "Why can't I move up

10

here? Why should we give it to *him*?" She didn't look at me.

"You're too young, Lily," Vic said. "You're best downstairs with us."

"*She* lived here," Lily said. Vic turned away abruptly. *Kathy*, I thought. "*She* wasn't that much older than I am now when *she* moved up here," Lily said. The words had the whiny singsong quality of frequent repetition. "I don't see why I can't—"

Vic cut her off. "That's enough, Lily."

A silence. Then, barely audible: "It's all wrong," Lily whispered.

"Well," I said. I found myself struggling with the desire to tell Lily she could visit me, and an equally strong—no, a stronger—desire to keep my mouth shut, to preserve the privacy I had only just realized I would have. Real gratitude to Vic and Julia filled me, for the first time. I turned to Vic. "I'd like to say hello to Julia," I said. "I thought I heard her before."

Vic's mouth tightened. "She'll say hello later, probably."

Probably. "Oh," I said.

Lily chortled obnoxiously, and then clapped a hand over her mouth.

I looked around again at the perfect little apartment. At Vic as he scraped away some bit of grit he'd suddenly noticed on the kitchen counter. At Lily, who had sprung up from the floor and gone to insinuate herself against Vic, who gave her an absentminded hug. At a stray slender shadow that flitted for the barest instant past the corner of my vision.

I was tired, okay, but I wasn't stupid. I didn't need a high-school diploma to figure out that Julia didn't want me there. Or Lily. But I had no choice. I was not welcome in Baltimore either. Davey had died when Emily did.

Now I was David, and I lived in Cambridge with strangers.

And shadows.

CHAPTER 2

No doubt partly because of the separateness of my living quarters, but also, I was sure, because it was her preference, I did not see my aunt Julia for two full days. She didn't even come to dinner my first evening, when Vic took Lily and me out to Harvard Square for burgers.

During those two days, Vic was away much of the time as well—he's an electrical contractor—and yet it was Julia's absence that I noticed as I unpacked and tried to settle in. To my knowledge, she didn't work. On the evening of my arrival, as I trudged upstairs with my boom box and CDs, I thought I heard her voice. But by the time I reached the landing, she'd retreated toward the back of the house. I kept listening after that, as with Vic's help I brought up the pieces of my computer, my TV and VCR, and armloads of clothes and videotapes, but I didn't hear her again. I certainly didn't go looking for her.

The next night, Vic gave me something that served as an explanation. He rapped on my door and came in, asked how the unpacking was going. Then he said, "Uh, in general, we all make do for ourselves around here. Even Lily. As you've got your own kitchen, Julia thought perhaps . . . she's quite busy, you see, and we've never been ones for formal family meals. And you are pretty much grown-up. I told her you'd want to take care of yourself, you'd appreciate your privacy . . ."

It took me a minute to understand what he was really saying. Then I said, "Of course. It's very considerate of you."

Vic avoided my eyes. He reached out tentatively and touched my shoulder. I knew—and he knew—that this was not what my mother had had in mind when she sent me to her brother's.

I was beginning to wonder if this really had been Vic's idea. Would my mother have lied about that to me? To my father? Or just to me?

"About money for food," Vic began.

I cut him off. "I have a credit card," I said. "And a bank account. My parents didn't want me to be a burden to you. It's no problem."

"But I'd like to give you—"

"No." I looked him straight in the eye. "Thank you, but no. You've been quite generous as it is." I busied myself arranging some stuff. After a few minutes Vic left, closing the door gently behind him. I thought he said something about seeing me later, but I couldn't be sure. There was a buzzing in my ears.

Emily, I thought. *Emily.*

14

I wondered, did Julia believe the tabloids were right about me, and the jury wrong? I wondered, had my parents pressured them to invite me? If so, how? But it sickened me to try to think about it. Did it matter? It was done. And it was only for a year. An academic year. Nine months. I would not look beyond that.

That night, I heard the oddest sound. It was a kind of . . . low *humming*—only just audible, somehow filled with urgency and . . . frustration? Whatever it was, it was definitely *not* tuneful. At first I was barely aware of it, and then, for one bare second, it swelled and seemed to fill my ears. I sat up in bed and turned on the light, briefly imagining—I don't know—a giant fly from a horror film? Something stupid, anyway; something nightmarish. But of course the room was empty in the harsh glare of electric light. And the sound, too, was suddenly gone: in fact my ears rang with silence. After a moment, I shrugged. I'd imagined quite a few strange things this last year. What was one more? And so I sank back into the semistupor that, these days, I called sleep.

Though I didn't see Julia, Lily was around. She parked herself on my sofa the next day and sullenly watched me unpack. Once, when I came back from transferring a pile of T-shirts to the bedroom bureau, I found her freely rooting around in a box of my books and papers.

"Lily," I said.

She looked up briefly, and then bent over the box again.

I said, "It's rude to go through other people's stuff."

Lily didn't change her position or look up. She

15

reached into the box and pulled out a large paperback. "Why is it rude?" she asked. She turned the book over and began to examine the back, and then I realized which one it was, and I panicked a little. I should have been more careful when I packed, but I hadn't thought anybody would be in my stuff. And I'd wanted to bring all my books. They'd become friends, that lonely year.

And that particular book, Emily had given me.

"Because everybody needs privacy," I said. I took the book from her. "And time alone. Do you understand?"

"No." Lily's eyes fixed on my face and scoured it inch by inch. It unnerved me.

"Look," I said, "you'd better leave. I want to unpack by myself." And, as she continued to kneel there on the floor, I walked to the open door and stood by it.

She waited just past the point at which I was sure she wasn't going to move. Then she got up, elaborately dusting off her knees. "Tell me something," she said, as if casually. "How did you feel when she went down?"

All the air left the room.

Lily was leaning forward, her gaze avid, sucking at mine. "Tell me. Did you feel . . . *powerful*? Were you glad? Even . . . just for a minute?"

I had words, somewhere inside me, but for a long moment they were formless. I thought, *She's a kid, she's just a kid*, but that didn't help. Greg and Emily and I had been kids too. Being under eighteen didn't mean you were innocent. Or harmless.

"Get out," I said.

Again she waited. Staring; challenging. And as I began to think that I would have to pick her up and remove her bodily—and I was abruptly prepared to do it—she lifted her chin and moved past me like a diva. Her feet thunked as she descended the stairs. I closed the door behind her. I leaned against it.

I heard my own breath come back in and out of my lungs. It sounded as if I'd been running.

CHAPTER 3

In my hand I felt the weight of Emily's book, and I remembered when she'd given it to me. To us. It hadn't been long after we'd first slept together, and she'd been so delighted with herself. She'd gleefully described her embarrassment at the bookstore; how she'd dallied and hung back in line to make sure she got a female cashier. How she'd also bought a couple of mysteries she didn't want, so that this book wouldn't be her only purchase.

We'd laughed so hard. And then she'd kissed me, coming in close, teasing, and I'd been as self-absorbed as an onion. Astounded at my luck and at the same time confident it was my due.

I was smug, beyond doubt. Maybe I was even dumb, not paying attention to anyone except myself. But I cared about Emily. We were good together. She was *not* frightened of me. I was *not* obsessive and jealous. I would *never* have hurt her. That wasn't me.

That wasn't me. Not then. Not now. Not ever. No.

But, still . . . still . . .

Slowly I became aware that my other hand hurt. For a long moment I could not unclench my fingers. Then, slowly, I could. My palm was bloody. I stared at it. My stomach lurched. I took in one deep breath, and then, carefully, another.

I would not think about Emily, or about Greg's compelling lies, or about my own doubts. I could not afford to.

And I could not afford to waste any emotion on Lily. Or on Julia. I was here in Cambridge. I had a job to do: a year of school to complete in a strange place, surrounded by new people who would at best be suspicious of me, and at worst—

No. I wouldn't think about that.

I moved to the bookcase and, working rapidly, filled the bottom shelves with my old science fiction books: Asimov, Bear, Bujold, Card, Heinlein, others. I tucked Emily's book, inappropriately, behind these other books that I needed to keep but knew I would probably not read again. Then I went to the sink to run cold water over my stinging hand.

I would be attending a private preparatory school called St. Joan's, which had once been an exclusive girls' school.

"But, ten years ago," Dr. Edythe Walpole, the headmistress, had said during the interview that my father arranged at the beginning of the summer, "we decided

19

to allow boys to enroll as well." She'd fixed me with a steady look over her half glasses.

I nodded. I didn't really care about the school's history. She had to know that.

"This is a small school," said Dr. Walpole. "Small and quiet. Fewer than a hundred students in each grade; classes with a low teacher-student ratio. We pride ourselves on the quality of our faculty; the depth of our courses. I teach a senior seminar in history, myself. Everyone who works here teaches, no matter what else they do."

Oh, really? I thought sourly. *The custodian too?* But I just nodded. I was hyperaware of my father, waiting outside the office, probably pacing. We'd flown up together from Baltimore that morning and were due to take another plane back in a couple of hours. "That sounds impressive," I said. I wondered how much my parents were planning to pay. Twice the normal tuition? More? Despite what the papers said, we weren't rich. How much would this year cost them, on top of all the legal fees?

Silence had fallen. I looked up and saw Dr. Walpole paging thoughtfully through my file. I knew what she was seeing there. The A's. The IQ number. The S.A.T. scores. Probably even the cross-country times. Davey was just about perfect, you see.

I waited. Finally she looked up, at me, at David. "Very well," she said. "We'll see how it goes."

I said, "Thank you." I wanted to say something else—there was a little silence in which I felt I was *expected* to say something else—but I couldn't think what.

In my attic apartment, I winced, remembering.

20

School would begin the next day. There would be countless such encounters to get through. Weeks, maybe months, to make myself blend into the walls. Settle everybody down. I would just have to do it. For the rest of my life, over and over, I would have to convince everyone—including me—of my harmlessness.

Nearly everything was unpacked. I decided to take a break, go for a walk. See if I could find some local stores. I needed a desk lamp. I needed to get out of the house for a while. I needed—badly—to run, and I would, as soon as I figured out where I'd put my running shoes.

I went down the stairs, through Vic and Julia's apartment, and down again. On the front porch, I nearly careened into a tall, skinny girl carrying a huge canvas. The artist, I guessed, who Vic had mentioned lived on the first floor. "Sorry," I said. We danced around each other; somehow, the girl managed to keep her grip on the unwieldy canvas.

Behind the canvas I caught a glimpse of her profile: dark skin, a high cheekbone, a sweep of brown hair tucked behind a lovely, delicate ear. Oddly penetrating, her eye stopped on me for an instant and my face flamed. She was beautiful, and she would think I— she'd have read the tabloids, heard what Greg had said . . .

I ducked my head to hide. The girl might have said something; I wasn't sure. I heard the rattle of her keys as she fumbled with them. Finally she got her door open and edged her canvas inside. I got just a glimpse of the interior of that first room, the living room, and it

21

astonished me almost out of my hideous self-consciousness. The room was completely empty.

Her door closed, softly.

After another second I looked over at her mailbox and read the name on it. An unusual name: Raina. Raina Doumeng.

CHAPTER 4

To my surprise, that evening I got a formal invitation to dinner. Vic knocked on my door to deliver it. "Julia is making a stew tonight," he said. "Why don't you come down at six?"

"Okay," I said, wondering if that meant she was just doing the cooking, and would therefore still not make an appearance. But when I came down that night, I found Julia in the kitchen, her back ramrod-straight, her hair shorter than I'd remembered and completely gray. She wore an apron fastened over casual clothes.

Tentatively, I approached and gave her a bouquet of late-summer wildflowers I'd found up the street at a little outdoor fruit and vegetable market. She seemed surprised, and, if not pleased, at least not actively hostile.

"Thank you, David," she said, my name sounding precise and measured. She examined me and then averted her eyes politely from my long hair, grown, defiantly, since my Eagle Scout appearance at the trial. She instructed Lily to find a vase for the flowers. "Then tell your father we'll be ready to eat in ten minutes."

Lily. All at once I could hear her unbelievable questions echo once again in my ears. I forced myself to glance at her, and found her watching me. I looked away.

Did you feel powerful?

She was a little girl. She could not have known what she was asking.

In a few minutes we all took our seats. Julia sat at the foot of the small, rectangular dining room table, Vic at the head, while Lily and I faced each other across the two sides. Julia had placed my flowers directly in the center of the table, making it difficult for me to see Lily.

And soon I felt slightly more relaxed. Julia was making an effort to be cordial, and Vic had ruffled Lily's hair affectionately just before we sat down, making her break out briefly in a smile.

Julia ladled out the stew, passing Vic's down to him via Lily, and we began eating.

"So, you start at St. Joan's tomorrow?" Julia asked me.

"Yes," I said. The stew was good; I complimented Julia on it and on the bread. She thanked me. There was a little silence.

"St. Joan's is a very good school," pronounced Julia finally. "I might send Lilian there when the time comes for her to attend high school. I don't want her to stay in public school when she's older. Because you never know. Gangs. Drugs."

Lily muttered something. I wondered briefly why

Lily was not attending parochial school now, as Kathy had, but then realized that it must be money. "There are probably scholarships for St. Joan's," I began, and then faltered as I met Julia's glare.

"I can afford to send Lilian to St. Joan's!" she snapped. "I don't need charity!"

"I didn't mean . . ." I let my voice drift off as Julia continued to glare, and I remembered that my father had offered to help with Kathy's college tuition, and been refused. And of course Kathy hadn't stayed long in college. I looked at Vic, hoping for help, but he was eating with great concentration, wiping the bowl with his bread, not looking up.

More silence. Like Vic, I attended to my dinner. Pretty soon I scraped bottom. I wanted more but the tureen was out of reach and somehow I was reluctant to ask Julia. The bread was nearby; I ate more of it. I turned my head to the right and examined the many family pictures collected in two large frames on the wall. I noted several of Lily, but I did not see Kathy's distinctive red hair.

Finally I couldn't stand the silence anymore. "Vic," I said, "are you a Patriots fan?"

Vic looked up. "Not really. I prefer baseball." He hesitated. "But maybe we could go to a game some weekend if you'd like."

"Sure," I said weakly, horrified. I did not want to go to a game with Vic; I had just been making conversation. "Sometime."

"Okay," said Vic. His eyes flickered away from mine, to the soup tureen, and then down to his own empty plate. He took a slice of bread from the basket.

25

Next, I tried a question about the house. This met with more response. Vic was seriously into home upkeep and repair. "These old wood frame houses repay the care," he said. He told me the history of the Boston double- and triple-deckers. "They're democratic, these houses," he said, looking around the room in satisfaction. "Some people think they're ugly,"—he squinted suspiciously at me—"all crammed together on a street. But I say this house has treated us well."

It was the perfect opening. "Vic," I said, "I was wondering about the skylights in the attic. Did you do something with them to diffuse the light differently?"

"A skylight's a skylight. What do you mean?"

"I don't know. Well, there's this shadow I see upstairs sometimes, in the late afternoon. It's tall, thin . . ." *Almost womanly*, I suddenly thought. "And well . . . anyway, I just wondered if maybe the light was funny. And also—" I was going to mention the humming, but Vic was frowning at me, shaking his head, and I stopped, uncertain.

"Also what?" Vic said.

I didn't want to go on, but I was stuck. "I . . . twice at night I've heard this noise . . . a buzz or a hum . . ." I stopped again. I thought I felt Lily's eyes on me, but when I looked across, her face was hidden behind the flowers.

Julia said, "Aren't you sleeping well? Why not?"

I could feel all their eyes. "I sleep fine," I said quickly. "It's just sometimes I hear this noise . . . I think it must be the wind."

"Yes," said Julia. "This is an old house, which you're—" Her eyes narrowed. "Not used to."

Vic nodded. "Old houses have personalities. Especially wooden houses. They creak."

"Oh," I said.

Silence again. Vic reached once more for the bread basket, but I had finished the last slice. I was still hungry. I had carried the tureen to the table for Julia, so I knew there was plenty more. I looked at Vic, and his plate, and then at my plate once more. I looked at Julia, who was patting her mouth with her napkin.

Suddenly I almost laughed. *Please, sir,* I thought, *I want some more.*

"Is there any more stew, Julia?" I said boldly. "I'd like seconds."

"Of course," said Julia. "Pass me your plate."

She didn't look at Vic. She didn't ask Vic if he also wanted seconds. She hadn't, I suddenly realized, said a word to Vic all evening. Or he to her. They hadn't exchanged a single glance, either.

I'm imagining things, I thought. Shadows, noises, atmosphere . . . I looked at Vic again, and Julia saw me do it. She said smoothly, "Lilian, ask your father if he'd like seconds."

I blinked. I received my plate back. Lily said, "Dad, would you like some more stew?"

"Yes, please, Lily," said Vic.

I watched as Vic passed his plate to Lily, who passed it on to Julia, who filled it generously and passed it back via Lily to Vic.

"Thank you," said Vic to Lily.

"He says thanks," said Lily to Julia.

"He's welcome," said Julia.

"She says you're welcome," said Lily to Vic.

27

I opened my mouth. Then I closed it. I looked from Vic to Julia. Vic was eating again and couldn't, wouldn't, meet my eyes. Julia did, though, for the barest second, before lifting her chin and looking away again.

No. I was *not* imagining this, at least. Vic and Julia weren't talking to each other. They were communicating through Lily.

Was I responsible for that, too?

I looked up and saw Lily, smiling sweetly at me. She had leaned sideways to have a good view.

"More bread?" she asked. "I can get you some from the kitchen."

"No," I said. "Thank you, but no."

CHAPTER 5

The next morning I went to school. It was a half day; I was supposed to register, pick up my class schedule, sign up for activities. It felt peculiar, getting ready for school by myself. The attic apartment was too quiet. As I ate cereal I remembered how my mother had always insisted on cooking a big breakfast for me on the first day of school. I remembered her ritual questions at dinner: *What were your impressions of your teachers today? Your classes?*

My father always had something more pointed to say. The same thing every year, delivered seriously and with full focus: *What are your goals this year, Davey?* I never got away with less than three.

Almost exactly a year before, I'd had a pocketful of conventional goals: grades and college applications and sports. And a new, unstated goal, just as orthodox, involving Emily. I'd been sure of getting whatever I wanted. I'd left the house early that morning and driven to Emily and Greg's to pick them up. We'd all crammed into the front seat. Greg, high, was full of noxious comments about everyone and everything. This may have been when Emily and I began to realize that he rarely *wasn't* high. He was utterly oblivious to the fact that Emily and I were holding hands. I'd known Emily always, of course—she was Greg's sister—but that summer . . . well. I'd wondered casually when she would get around to telling him. Or if he would ever notice on his own. Greg was ten months older than Emily, but that summer he had begun to seem like the younger sibling.

You were my *friend first,* he said to me later. Like a spoiled child.

I wrenched my mind from a picture of Greg's hate- and despair-filled face the last time I had seen him. In the courtroom, sitting next to his parents, listening as I was acquitted of killing his sister. Maybe he called me jealous—obsessive—violent—because that was how he felt. I don't know.

On the stand, his hands shook.

I pushed away my cereal. It was time to leave.

I went downstairs quietly, half expecting to find the first-day-of-school rituals being played out with Lily. But Lily's bedroom door was closed and I remembered that her school didn't begin until the following Monday. Maybe her parents would be talking to each other by then.

Vic had given me directions from North Cambridge to the Charles River, where St. Joan's was, and I drove there easily enough, parking in the small student lot. I got out of my car and watched my new classmates pour off a city bus and amble toward the stretch of buildings. At my old school, in the suburbs of Baltimore, most of the seniors had driven. It didn't look to be that way here. Should I ask Vic about bus routes tonight? Even the thought depressed me. As long as I had my car, I had the illusion of an easy escape. Anyway, there was no sense trying to fit in.

I had expected to feel lonely, but I didn't. I felt detached.

I walked past idle clumps of talking kids and went through the main doors of the school. The packet I'd been mailed said to report to the cafeteria. I did that. I stood in line before a table marked T THROUGH Z, and waited my turn, watching, listening to the hubbub around me. Finally I got to the front of the line. When I said my name, the woman looked up at me, something she hadn't done with the kids before me. But her hands riffled automatically through the box and whipped out a piece of paper. "Here you go, Mr. Yaffe." I might have imagined the emphasis on my name.

"Thanks," I said politely, and turned away.

I reported to another table and got my free St. Joan's T-shirt. It had white lettering on a dark pink background. For a few seconds I thought about advising Dr. Walpole that she'd have more success recruiting boys if the school colors changed. Ha. Like I cared.

There were tables for clubs and activities. When I saw the one for cross-country, my stomach tightened. But I walked up, nodded to the girl behind the table, and signed my name to a list. And then, as I turned away, I saw the skinhead.

31

He was easily six and a half feet tall, and thin as a flagpole. He wore heavy laceless combat boots without socks, camouflage shorts, and the pink, glaringly new St. Joan's T-shirt. His white head bobbed precariously on a reedlike neck as his watery blue eyes scanned the room. Briefly, as if feeling my gaze, his eyes met mine and then slid down to the schedule clutched between bony fingers.

He stood alone in the cafeteria. The students parted smoothly before him and rejoined behind, as if he were Moses at the Red Sea.

I turned back to the cross-country table and said to the girl, "Excuse me, but who is that?"

She followed my gaze and her mouth twisted a little. "Oh. Frank Delgado."

The fact was, you didn't see a lot of guys my age who shaved their heads. When you did, they didn't wear combat gear. Unless . . .

"Is he . . ." I paused, not certain whether I wanted to say it. But the girl caught my drift and finished for me.

". . . really a skinhead?" I nodded, and she shrugged. "Who knows? He's a weirdo, that's for sure. New last year." And with that she seemed for the first time really to see me. Her face brightened with interest; she leaned forward and smiled. "Hey, you're new too, aren't you? I've never seen you before. I'm Michelle Grafton. I'm a junior. What's your name? What year are you?"

Before I could reply she grabbed the clipboard and looked at where I had signed my name. There was a little pause. Odd how even the top of someone's head can be expressive.

"David Bernard Yaffe," I said distinctly.

She looked up. Her mouth was frozen in a little O. I gave her a warm smile. "Nice to meet you, Michelle," I said. She quailed.

I felt like Dracula. It was not entirely unpleasant.

CHAPTER 6

I had nothing else to do at school, but I didn't want
to go back to Vic and Julia's. I left my car in the
student lot and walked the half mile to Harvard
Square. There I walked some more, listening to street
musicians, reading posted restaurant menus, finally settling for a couple of slices of pizza. I went into a big
discount bookstore called Wordsworth and browsed
their science fiction section. I bought a CD at Tower
Records. I watched *Blade Runner* at the Brattle Theater.

When the movie ended, it was nearly seven o'clock.
I got my car, stopped at the Star Market for groceries,
and arrived back at Vic and Julia's just as dusk was
settling into full dark. All over the neighborhood, lights
were on, illuminating the rooms and people within. Vic
and Julia's windows gleamed softly above my head. I
realized then that I had hoped they wouldn't be home.
I did not want to talk to them.

On the porch, I looked at the dark windows of the

first-floor apartment where Raina Doumeng lived. I wondered if she really had recognized me. I wondered if even now the girl from the track table was telling her friends about meeting me. I wondered why the skinhead at school chose to expose his differentness so openly.

As quietly as possible I went upstairs to the second floor. The television blared in the Shaughnessy kitchen at the back, and I heard the soft clink of cutlery on a plate. I headed up the hall toward the attic stairs.

Vic and Julia's bedroom door was closed. Lily's was open, however, and I was unable to pass it without looking in. On the bed, Lily was lying on her stomach with her chin on her hands, staring at the doorway, at me, as I went by. No book, no music to occupy her. And no expression on her face, not even boredom. As we looked at each other for a split second, her expression did not change, even as I forced myself to nod at her.

Lily. Speaking of different.

The attic felt like a haven. If only I didn't have to go through Vic and Julia's to reach it.

I unpacked the groceries and then my backpack, tossing the St. Joan's T-shirt to the floor. Below, I fancied that Lily was now staring up at me through the ceiling. Automatically, my eyes calculated the exact spot on the floor below which she was located.

Ridiculous. I was being ridiculous. And it was undoubtedly because I was hungry. I went and got the crackers and peanut butter, but I'd bought salt-free, fat-free, cholesterol-free crackers by mistake. I threw the box away and ate some peanut butter out of the jar. I put on a CD but then, impatiently, turned the boom box off. I listened to the silence. Tomorrow there would be classfuls of Michelle Graftons. And in each class, a roll call in which I must respond to my name.

There was nothing I could do about that. Nothing I could do about anything.

My phone rang. It was my mother, with a modified version of first-day-of-school questions. My father was still at work, she said. I accepted the excuse, or pretended to.

As soon as she slowed down, I cut in. I couldn't help it. "Did Vic and Julia really invite me here?" I demanded. "Or did you engineer it?"

"What?"

"Whose idea was it in the first place, to have me come here?"

There was a telltale moment of silence. Then: "What does it matter whose idea it was? David, I assure you, Vic was only too happy . . ."

I doubted that. "Well, Julia is not happy," I said. "And if you want to break up Vic's marriage, this might do it." I didn't say, *And imagine how I feel*. She clearly wasn't interested in that.

My mother said, "What are you talking about? What about Julia?"

"Julia is not happy about my being here," I repeated. "She's so mad at Vic about it, she's not talking to him. And he's not talking to her. And," I added, suddenly inspired, "if that's not enough, think of Lily. They're making her be the go-between. It's not psychologically healthy for a kid. I'm messing them all up. I shouldn't be here."

"Vic and Julia aren't talking to each other?"

My mother is not usually slow. "That's right," I said

36

patiently. And I told her about the dinner. I gave her the long version, with details: the way she likes her information. Then I paused. "Hello?" I said finally.

"I'm thinking," said my mother.

I waited another minute. "Look," I said, "you do see that my being here is messing them up and that it's not comfortable for me, knowing—" I stopped. I didn't want to go on.

"We had this conversation," my mother said. I could hear the strain in her voice. "You need to finish high school. Nothing has changed. Not for you. Or us.

"As to Vic and Julia," my mother continued, when it was clear I wasn't going to say anything, "I know you will find this difficult to believe, but I suspect . . . well, I doubt their quarrel is about you."

"Really," I said.

"Really," said my mother. "I've had a feeling for a few years now that things weren't right. From what Vic has said—or maybe hasn't said . . ." She sighed. "I didn't want to know about it, but I did. Things haven't been right for Vic and Julia for a very long time. Since Kathy died, at least."

With that, I remembered the dining room wall downstairs. Not a single photo of Vic and Julia's older daughter.

"It's not you, David," continued my mother. "You're not . . . you can't make things worse for them than they already were. Are." She sighed again.

Maybe she was right. Maybe I wasn't the problem. But how could my mother think my presence wouldn't make things worse? I was suddenly overwhelmed with tiredness. It was terrible, I suppose, if my uncle and aunt had come apart over Kathy. Worse, obviously, than if they had recently fought only about me. But I didn't care.

"Look," I started again. I wasn't clear what my point was, what I wanted. I guess I knew I couldn't leave; knew there was nowhere to go. But I needed her to hear me.

Instead my mother burst in with a torrent of words. "I'm just so glad you're there for them, David. My poor big brother. And little Lily. Even Julia, she can't help who she is. Maybe you can help them.

"Listen," said my mother. "Maybe in a little while Vic will be able to talk to you. Oh, I know he won't really talk, but, you know, that male bonding thing. You can bond. It could really help Vic, that you're there. Even if he can't talk about Kathy."

I couldn't believe I was hearing this. Didn't she—my God, she was my mother!—didn't she understand a single thing about me? About what had happened to me? "Mom," I started.

But she cut me off. "David, I don't think Vic would have offered to have you if he didn't want you. You're family. Vic always wanted a son."

I already have a father, I thought, but I couldn't say that. I tried to say something—anything—else, but could not.

There was no way to explain that I wasn't the kind of person Vic would want as a son. That the thought of more family bonds—more people to disappoint—terrified and angered me. Even if there had been, there was no one to listen or understand. No one in this world.

I suppose I had never really thought there was.

CHAPTER 7

The skinhead—Frank Delgado—was in my senior history seminar. On the first day of class he wore the same camouflage shorts with the now-limp pink T-shirt. He sat down at the front of the room, propped his legs up on a desk beside him, and closed his eyes. Against the backdrop of the chalkboard, his bald head gleamed as if he'd polished it. He did not polish his boots, however. They were encrusted with dried mud.

It was the last class of the day, and I had arrived early—right before Delgado—and sat down at the back of the small classroom. The rest of the kids, as they trickled in, appeared to find this distribution a problem. They chose seats clustered together in the middle of the room. They talked to each other, but were conscious of me. They stole glances at me whenever they dared. Delgado they ignored.

When I had a choice, I was and always had been the

kind of kid who sat at the back. It made even more sense here; once class was in session, everyone would be facing forward and not looking at me. But after a few minutes I stood up and moved to the seat on the other side of the skinhead.

I couldn't tell you why.

I had spent another uneasy night. Despite the fact that I hadn't been aware of sleeping, I had a confused dream in which Emily chased me down the corridors of my old high school. She was laughing, and so was I, but I was also terrified and I knew I needed to keep running. If she caught me she was going to tell me something I didn't want to know. Then she grabbed me by the arm from behind, and her strength was extraordinary. She swung me around hard, slamming my back against the lockers. And it was not Emily anymore. It was Lily. Lily, hair aflame. Powerful, angry, demanding. And somehow also . . . crying.

At that point I'd known for sure that I was dreaming, known also that I was close enough to the surface to wake up. It was then I'd heard the humming again, insistent. And I'd opened my eyes in the gray dawn.

For a second in the doorway across the bedroom I saw that shadow again—but this time it was distinctly human. A girl—a woman. I struggled up onto my elbows and said fuzzily, frantically: *"Emily? Emily!"* even though I knew, I *knew,* it was not Emily. But then the shadow had . . . not disappeared, but *dissolved.*

And the humming had stopped.

In short, it had been a nasty night, a rotten preliminary to my first day of classes.

I glanced sideways at Frank Delgado, glad of his presence as a distraction. What was this raggedly dressed skinhead kid doing at an exclusive prep school? Was it really that difficult for Dr. Walpole to enroll boys? Of course, she'd enrolled me. Probably the skinhead had a desperate family, too, willing to pay any price.

The bell rang, and a minute passed, and it was only then that the teacher entered, at a pace a shade faster than brisk. Next to me, Frank Delgado withdrew his feet from the neighboring desk and casually angled to face the front. The teacher put some books down and moved to sit behind her desk. It was only then that I saw who it was: Dr. Walpole. I glanced down at my schedule. Yes, there it was: Sr Hist Sem Medv. Walpl.

I remembered now, she had said she taught history. But I hadn't expected to find her teaching *me*. It made me feel . . . watched. I sank down a little in my chair.

Dr. Walpole's gaze moved rapidly, comprehensively, from face to face. "Senior seminar in medieval history," she said. "Yearlong, three credits. Everybody in the right place?"

Everybody was. "Good," said Dr. Walpole. "Maybe you'll all move up into the first and second rows, then, to indicate your intense interest in the subject. We shouldn't need to use the last two rows at all. Come on." Slowly, the rest of the students moved, filling in the desks beside and behind Frank Delgado and me.

Possibly Dr. Walpole was being kind. Possibly this was simply her usual mode of operation. Whatever, I didn't care for it.

At three-thirty, I escaped to my car. I'd parked facing

41

the school, with a view of the front entrance, and as I turned the engine on, I spotted Frank Delgado coming out. I continued to watch as he made his solitary way across Memorial Drive and loped down along the Charles River.

If I'd been home, I would have talked about him that night at the dinner table. "There's this kid, a skinhead, in one of my classes," I would have said. My parents would have been very interested. But then, if I'd been home, I'd have already known all about him. I had been thoroughly entrenched in the information circles at my old school.

I went back to the Shaughnessy house. I had homework to do. Calculus would be easy for quite a while; I'd done it the year before. Same with several other subjects. But Dr. Walpole wasn't teaching history out of a textbook; instead, she was assigning a lot of primary source reading. That night's was on the medieval church hierarchy. Thrilling.

On the porch beside the front door, Vic had nailed up a new mailbox for me. In it was a large manila envelope from my mother. I ripped open the envelope and found some college applications. Stanford. University of Chicago. Dartmouth. My mother had attached a short note:

> *Dear David,*
> *I've written to all the schools on our list from last year and given them your new address. Here are the applications that had already arrived here. If more come, I'll send them on, of course.*
> *Best love.*

She had also included newspaper clippings from *The Washington Post*: a series about the college application process and the pressures on Young People Today. I grimaced, and then stuffed everything back into the envelope. I was staring down at it when I felt a presence at my elbow. Lily.

It was time to forgive her for what she'd said to me about Emily. She was just a kid; she couldn't have known what she was saying. I opened the door and gestured her inside in front of me. We mounted the stairs. I reached for conversation. "Wasn't today your first day back at school? How's sixth grade so far?"

"Rotten." Lily opened the door of her parents' apartment with her key.

"Care to elaborate?" I asked. I wanted to go on up to the attic, but felt uneasy leaving Lily. Where was Julia? She didn't work. Shouldn't she be home to greet Lily?

"Nah." Lily bounced on into the living room. After a second the television sang out in a commercial. Reluctantly, I followed her. Lily had flung herself onto the carpet in front of the TV and was wielding the remote control with an expert hand, rapidly flicking from channel to channel and finally settling on a cartoon, *Scooby Doo*.

"Lily?" I had to raise my voice. "Lily!"

She didn't turn. "What?"

"Where's Jul—your mother?"

"She has her O.A. meeting at four today."

"O.A.?"

"Overeaters Anonymous."

"What?" I said. "She's not fat. Did she used to be?"

Lily was concentrating on the TV. "No, she just likes

43

the people there. She says they've all suffered deeply and they have great strength. It's uplifting to hear them." Lily restored her attention to the TV, and I thought she was finished, but then she added: "Mom goes to G.A. and A.A., too. They're sort of the same thing, only different. You know?"

Gamblers Anonymous. Alcoholics Anonymous. "You okay down here by yourself?" I asked.

"Oh, puh-leeze." Lily rolled her eyes. Relieved that at least she and I had been able to talk, I retreated upstairs as the TV yelled, "Good boy, Scooby! You unmasked the ghost!"

I don't know when Julia or Vic got home.

CHAPTER 8

Three or four weeks went by. I did my school-work more or less diligently, but could not make myself actually show up for cross-country practice. Instead, I began running by myself every day after school. I chose a five-mile route that circled through North Cambridge and then looped around the Fresh Pond reservoir. While I ran, I wore headphones and thought about nothing. It felt good. Sometimes I ran the loop twice.

Yom Kippur came. I didn't intend to fast; I had not fasted since my bar mitzvah year. But somehow or other I forgot to eat until just a few hours before sun-set, and then I thought, why not hang on? So I did. It was just a test of will. It meant nothing. I didn't go to synagogue. I didn't feel cleansed. I didn't feel forgiven.

One October afternoon I came home after my run to find Vic stacking a half cord of wood in the backyard against the house. He nodded at me, and I took off my headphones and joined him, ignoring his protests. We went back and forth from the base of the driveway, where the wood had been dumped, to the back of the house. I found myself glancing at Raina Doumeng's first-floor windows for signs of her presence. Nothing.

"Hard to believe this'll be needed," I said idly, nodding at my armload of firewood. It was a perfect Indian summer day, about seventy degrees.

Vic shrugged. "Believe it. It gets plenty cold around here, though we haven't gotten a lot of snow the past couple of years. Thank God. I hate shoveling."

"I'll do it this year," I said.

"I didn't mean—"

"I know." I finished stacking my current load. "Don't worry about it. Least I can do."

"But—"

"Think of what my mother would say if I didn't pull my weight around here."

"Eileen." A smile lightened Vic's eyes for an instant, and then disappeared. "Okay. You do the shoveling."

We continued working in silence, and as the stack neared completion, I wondered if my mother would consider this a bonding experience. She had called regularly every Sunday morning with her pick for Congressional Idiocy of the Week, a list of books I ought to read, gossip about my father's activities, and a few carefully worded questions about my life. Then, just before hanging up, she'd ask, as if casually, "And Vic? What's new with Vic and Julia?"

Each week I considered telling her to leave me alone and call Vic herself. But I never did.

". . . been thinking about installing a woodstove up

on the third floor, too," Vic was saying. "But I'm not sure if there's enough clearance."

"No, I don't think there is," I said. There was nothing wrong with a conventional heating system. "I'm sure it'll be warm enough without one."

Vic adjusted the last few logs on top of his stack. "Well, yes, I put in insulation, but a home needs a fire. I'd always planned—"

I interrupted him. The last thing I wanted was Vic cozying up the apartment for me. "Vic, there's something I've been meaning to ask you."

Vic blinked. "What?"

"My mother says they're thinking about driving up here for Thanksgiving."

For a moment, he didn't seem quite able to take it in. "Eileen and Stuart? Here?"

"Yeah." I watched his eyes slide away from mine, back to the woodpile. His left cheek twitched. "She says she'll roast a turkey in my oven," I said. "Invite you and Julia and Lily up."

I wasn't thrilled with the idea either; in truth I didn't know whether I wanted them to come or not. But Vic looked as if the entire woodpile had fallen on him.

"They'd be staying with me, so if Julia . . ." I stopped. I couldn't go any further. It would be presumptuous. In fact, the whole situation was ridiculous. Two or three frozen turkey dinners while watching football on TV—alone—was a far superior holiday plan. Except what if Vic and Julia then felt compelled to invite me to their table? "Anyway, she wondered what you'd think," I finished.

"Oh," said Vic. He cleared his throat. "Well. It would

be good for Lily to see her aunt and uncle. It's been . . ." He set his jaw and continued. "Four years."

I nodded. I thought he was done. I opened my mouth—

"Four years since Kathy died," Vic said. His voice was unexpectedly loud, almost defiant. I realized this was the first time I'd heard him say her name since I'd moved in. Even Lily—on the one occasion she'd referred to Kathy—had said *she*. "It doesn't seem so long, does it?" Vic said. He stood up straight, as if he expected a medal.

And I felt myself tighten with anger. I knew this conversation was exactly what my mother wanted between Vic and me. I knew I ought to feel sympathy for him. For them all. I knew I ought to want to help.

I just didn't. What had happened in that family, what was happening now—it wasn't my business and I didn't want to be part of it. I had my own stuff.

I didn't answer. After a few uncomfortable moments, Vic went on. "Maybe I'll call Eileen about Thanksgiving. Do you think that's a good idea?"

"Why don't you talk to your wife first?" I said nastily. Vic stared at me. "Oh, I don't mean a *real* conversation. You can have Lily ask Julia about it, and then Julia can send Lily back to you with a reply."

"David—" Vic stopped. My words sat in the silence. I wasn't sorry. For a long, long moment I wasn't sorry at all. Then Vic turned away.

"Look," I said quickly. "I didn't mean to say that. It's not my business." Vic turned back toward me, slowly.

"Forget it," I said. "I've gotta go do some work. See you later, Vic, okay?"

I could feel Vic's eyes following me as I disappeared around the side of the house. I was still angry, but at myself now, as well as at Vic.

I went upstairs to the attic. After spending twenty minutes reading about the differences between Gothic and Byzantine cathedrals, I heard a loud knocking at the lower door. And a call: "David? Can I speak with you?"

Vic. After a moment, I went down the stairs and opened the door. "I'm sorry about what I said before," I said, blocking the doorway with my body. "But can we talk about it another time? I'm studying—"

Vic waved a hand apologetically, but he didn't move. "It won't take long." He looked off into space for a second. "Please."

I moved aside. We climbed the stairs, and Vic pulled out a dinette chair. He moved as if to sit down, but then changed his mind and instead stood awkwardly behind it, grasping the back. I stood a few feet away, unsure what to do.

Not looking at me, Vic said, "About me and Julia. I realize it must seem strange to you . . ." He trailed off. Then: "I've never spoken about this before."

I wished he still wasn't speaking about it. "There's no need to explain anything to me."

Vic ignored me. "I didn't want Eileen to know," he said. "I can't imagine what I was thinking. With you living here . . ."

He took a deep breath. I looked at him. He released

49

the chair and pulled at his hair instead. Then, finally, he sat down. "This wasn't what I meant to talk about." He waved at the other chair. "Could you sit down, please? I can't talk with you looming over me."

I sat.

"I didn't think your being here would matter much," Vic said at last. "I just wanted to do something for Eileen. But it has made a difference . . ."

"I'm sorry—" I began, but Vic waved me into silence.

He wasn't looking at me. "I guess you know that Julia and I . . . we don't really see much of each other these days. We've sort of fallen into . . . I don't think it's so unusual. A lot of people—a lot of couples—when you've been married a long time . . ."

Vic paused again, then finally went on, his face still averted. "I kind of stopped noticing how we lived. But then you moved in. Just your being here has changed things. Even if you left—it's too late. We can't go back now. We can't . . . we can't be comfortable again."

"You want me to move out," I said flatly.

Vic looked shocked. "No! No, I was just saying . . . I realize that you think you're the problem here, David, but it's not you. It's Kathy. It was always Kathy."

"Oh," I said. I felt acutely uncomfortable.

Vic rubbed at his face. He said to his hands, "Julia thought we should have been stricter . . . Especially after Kathy dropped out of college. But I said let her live her own life." He shrugged. "Julia thinks it was my fault, what happened. She says I always under-

50

mined her. I never showed a united front." He lapsed into silence.

"Oh," I said again.

"So, does Eileen know?" Vic asked abruptly. "About Julia and me? About . . . about how we live?"

I felt like a snitch. "Yeah."

"Maybe I'm glad," Vic said softly. He got up, his movements suddenly decisive. "You invite your parents for Thanksgiving, David. You do that. It'll be good to see them, good to talk. I'll tell Julia—" He met my eyes and smiled briefly, unhappily. "I'll tell her myself."

Happy Thanksgiving, I thought sourly. I said, "Okay."

Vic dropped his hand on my shoulder. "I'll talk to Julia myself," he repeated, as if he needed to promise. "We have to move forward. We have to stop having Lily talk for us."

I nodded. I got up to accompany him to the door. "That's probably best for Lily, too," I said hesitantly.

Vic stopped midtread and frowned at me, puzzled. "Best for Lily? What do you mean?"

I blinked, equally confused. "Just—I just meant that it must be uncomfortable for her, being in the middle."

Vic looked surprised. "We love Lily," he said. "It's the one thing Julia and I agree on. Lily knows that. She knows she doesn't have anything to do with our fight."

For one very long moment my mind went completely blank. I was no authority on psychology, but . . .

Vic was still looking at me. "Don't you think Lily knows she's loved?"

"Of course," I said. "I'm sure she does."

"That's all that matters," Vic said, satisfied. He went on downstairs. I followed and closed the door behind him.

A wisp of a Beatles song floated past my inner ear: *All you need is love.*

Ha. In the middle of a frightful marriage, Vic still believed it. Naiveté? Strength? Stupidity? It didn't matter why. He did.

From my distance, I envied him his belief, even though I knew with my whole soul that he was wrong.

Dead wrong.

CHAPTER 9

Although Frank Delgado was in only one of my classes, it didn't take me long to confirm that he was exactly the outcast he appeared to be. He sat alone in the cafeteria, walked alone through the halls. He even ignored—or was ignored by—the other misfits.

Dr. Walpole liked him, however. More than liked, I soon realized: valued. "What do you think so far, Mr. Delgado?" she asked him at the end of a class in the sixth week of school, just after the bell rang. It was a quirk of hers to address all her students formally.

Most of the other kids had bolted for the door. But Frank had only just completed the process of standing up. He always moved with concentration, as if an unplanned motion might inadvertently disconnect an arm or foot.

I began idly rearranging the contents of my backpack. I was not going to miss this. I hadn't yet heard the skinhead utter a complete sentence. He never volunteered an answer, never participated in discussion. And Dr. Walpole did not prompt him, or try to draw him in. This despite the fact that she didn't permit anyone else in class to disengage.

He didn't seem to be mentally handicapped. I had wondered about that at first, until I saw the books he toted around and pulled out whenever he had a spare moment. He had a way of hunching over a book so that you usually couldn't tell what it was, but a couple of times I had caught sight of titles. *The Book of Mormon.* Poems of Paul Celan. *Vathek.* Perhaps most bizarrely: *Diana: Her True Story.*

I couldn't help wondering why Dr. Walpole did leave him so thoroughly alone in class. The class was too small for it not to be noticed. And nobody liked Frank for it. How had Dr. Walpole missed that? She wasn't doing the guy any favors.

"Well, are you bored yet, Mr. Delgado? Please, don't hold back on my account." Dr. Walpole's voice was dry and slightly amused.

Instead of speaking, Frank glanced at me. Dr. Walpole followed his eyes. There was a little silence, and I felt my jaw tighten. What was the big deal? It wasn't as if Dr. Walpole had asked him for the password to the Fort Knox computers. "Yeah," I said to Frank Delgado. "I'd like to know too. You bored, buddy?"

"No," said Frank Delgado. His watery eyes focused on me; I felt like a bacterium beneath an electron microscope. "I'm not bored. You are."

It was as if Dr. Walpole weren't there. I was the first

to blink. And when I did the skinhead added, just as expressionlessly, "And scared."

If he wanted to get me to leave, he couldn't have chosen his words better. I picked up my backpack and walked out of the room. And as I left I heard him shout, unexpectedly, after me.

"Hey, Yaffe! What are you going to do about it? Anything?"

Oddly, the tone wasn't challenging. It was merely . . . curious.

CHAPTER 10

"It's all settled for Thanksgiving," my mother said the following Sunday. But she gave no details of her conversation with Vic, instead concentrating on how big a turkey she planned to buy and how she would transport it from Baltimore in a cooler. "Uh-huh," I said, and found myself hoping the humming shadow would keep herself quiet while my parents were there. If I were to hear and see her in their presence—and they didn't . . . I couldn't bear the thought.

I spent the rest of the morning running my daily loop around North Cambridge. Afterward, I bought a newspaper, and ate two donuts and drank three coffees at Verna's Coffee Shop.

I was finishing up a satisfying mental list of the peculiarities of Frank Delgado when I came to and found myself staring, pen in hand, at the Sunday crossword. I got up from my table and left Verna's, heading to the Shaughnessy house.

Lily was raking leaves in the tiny front yard. Her head was down, and I watched her plod to the sidewalk, place her rattan rake on the edge of the grass and then turn away, grasping the rake handle with both hands behind her. She paused for a moment as if gathering her strength, and then walked the twelve-foot width of the yard with the rake bouncing along behind, dropping as many leaves as it gathered.

I didn't like Lily. I couldn't like Lily. For reasons I couldn't—or wouldn't—pinpoint, she made me uneasy. But right then she reminded me of myself at her age, doing chores as slowly and inefficiently as possible and hoping for early release. It made me smile. The smile felt strange on my face. "Do you get time off for good behavior?" I asked.

Her head shot up. I glimpsed her glare for an instant before she began another trek across the lawn. Behind her, the rake barely skimmed the ground. I went over to the front stoop and sat down to watch.

"Lily, have you ever seen the movie *Conan the Barbarian*?" I asked, after a few minutes. "There's a scene where Arnold Schwarzenegger is enslaved at the mill. He walks around and around, year after year, pulling a two-ton grindstone and building his muscles."

Lily dropped the rake. She turned to face me, hands on her hips. "So?"

"So you remind me of Arnold," I said. "Hard at work."

Lily turned her back again and bent to get the rake.

I sighed. "Hey, would you like some help? We could make a pile for you to jump in."

"No. My father asked *me* to rake. He didn't ask you."

"I'm sure he wouldn't mind." I waited. "Come on, Lily. It's always more fun with someone else."

Her look said she doubted it. I shrugged, and went off to the toolshed in the back, where I found another rake; old, metal, and heavy. I began cleaning up after Lily. A few minutes later, I tried once more: "Do you want to make a pile? We can borrow some leaves from next door."

"It would just make more leaves to bag."

I gave up. We finished the raking. Lily held open a large garbage bag for the leaves while I stuffed them in. Up and down the street, neighbors had packed their leaves into orange and black jack-o'-lantern bags to make Halloween displays, but the Shaughnessy bags were the regular kind, plain brown paper, destined for immediate disposal.

"I guess that's it." I brushed my hands off on my jeans and reached over to pick up the rakes. "I'll just put these away."

"I'll do that."

"No, really, it's—"

"I said *I* would do it," Lily burst out. Her face was reddening. "*I'm* going to do it!"

I held out my hands. "Hey—"

She grabbed the rakes, nearly staggering under the unexpected weight of the metal one before managing to steady herself, propping the ends of both rakes against the ground and keeping them upright with her hands, leaning her weight into them. "You're always interfering! Why don't you mind your own business? Why did you come here, anyway? We didn't want you!"

"Lily—"

"I wish you'd leave!" She was panting. Involuntarily, I took a step back from her. She was clearly on the edge of hysteria.

"Lily," I began, "I just want—"

She cut me off again. "I don't care what you want! Why should I? What *I* want, that's what matters!" She was shaking with rage, and a sound—almost a growl—emerged from her throat. Her hands tightened around the rakes, and she tried to throw them at me. But while she might have been able to hurl the rattan rake, the other one was too heavy for her. It slipped from her hand as she raised it and fell with a thunk to the ground between us, the rattan rake falling feebly next to it.

We both looked at the rakes on the ground. Then Lily turned away. I heard her gasping for breath, saw her shoulders rise and fall. But I was afraid to try to comfort her. I had no idea what this was about, or what I had done to set her off. I couldn't tell if she was already crying or was struggling to hold tears back.

I prayed neither Vic nor Julia would come outside and find us like this.

Finally Lily managed to calm down. Even though a big part of me thought it would be better to say nothing, I couldn't stop myself. "Lily, what have I done to make you so angry?"

Lily mumbled.

"I'm sorry. I can't hear you," I said.

This time she flung the words over her shoulder. "Why were you talking to my father about me?"

What did she mean? Then I remembered.

Lily had turned to face me. Her fists were clenched. She had not been crying. She was not near tears.

She said fiercely, "Aren't you going to answer me?"

I tried to fumble my way. "Lily, I'm sorry. Your father and I were just discussing Thanksgiving. You came up . . ." For some reason I felt like I was getting myself in deeper. I switched my approach. "What did your father tell you we'd said?"

"He was talking to my *mother*," Lily said. Her voice was filled with . . . disbelief? Astonishment? Pain? All of them. "Not to me." She flashed me a look of hatred. "About Thanksgiving. About your parents coming." Her tone made it plain they were about as welcome as I was. "I heard it."

"Yes," I said. "My parents will be staying upstairs with me, but we'll all have Thanksgiving dinner together." I weighed whether to tell her I didn't particularly want my parents to come either, but decided against it. "They're looking forward to seeing you."

The expression on Lily's face made me stop talking. "You interrupted me," she said.

I opened my mouth to apologize, and then closed it. When had control slipped from me to Lily? She was standing there, facing me, perfectly self-possessed despite her rage.

She waited until she was sure I wouldn't interrupt her again. Then she said, "You told my father to talk to my mother instead of me." She leaned forward suddenly. *"Didn't you?"*

The answer popped from my mouth. "Yes," I said.

Lily caught her breath. "I knew it was your fault."

My fault. I was very, very tired of everything being my fault. "Lily," I said. I leaned over and took her firmly by the shoulders. "Listen to me."

Lily tried to twist away. She kicked out, hard, just missing my crotch. Then she clawed for my eyes. I had to grab her hands, her arms, try to hold her away. "Hey," I said, "calm down. Calm down! Will you just calm—"

She spat in my face.

I caught myself a split second before slapping her.

I was holding Lily with my left hand, and actually had my right hand upraised to strike. My stomach roiled. *Reflex.* It's the body's betrayal of the mind. It's only a reflex.

As if that mattered. As if I were someone who could dismiss a reflex as "only."

I lowered my hand. I gave Lily's shoulder a very awkward pat. It was stiff. I stepped back, away from her, away from myself. "Lily, I'm sorry," I said. "I would never hit you."

She froze at my words, almost seeming to need a moment to translate them. Then the rancor disappeared from her face as if it had been wiped off with a clean wet rag. She looked at my lowered hand; at my face.

She leaned forward with the intensity of a drill sergeant. Her eyes filled with . . . *something.* She said, softly, so softly, *"Are you sure?"* And in my head I heard her other question, from before: *Did you feel powerful?*

For a moment I had the insane conviction that Lily had intimate knowledge of all my worst nightmares.

Then I recovered. I glared at her. "Yes," I said. "I'm sure."

She stared gravely back at me. Then, incongruously, the corner of her mouth twitched. She put her hand over her mouth and laughed outright, once, in a short bark. And then the laughter seemed to seize her body and take possession; it rocked her frame and escaped from her mouth in great peals that somehow did not sound amused. She laughed as if it hurt; as if she would never stop.

Then, abruptly, she did stop. And looked at me, her eyes still filled with that . . . *something*.

I couldn't bear it. I turned. I left. I walked.

I did not run.

CHAPTER 11

That evening, I turned on my computer and went online for hours, reading alt.tv.x-files, downloading software, surfing the Web. But in the end I could no longer avoid thinking. Lily's frightening laughter—my hand—her question—the look in her eyes—my hand.

My upraised hand.

Did you feel powerful?

Sometimes in my head I can still hear the snap of Emily's neck.

One day toward the end of the trial my father grabbed me by both shoulders. In a distant way I was astonished. I had never seen him other than contained, measured. But that afternoon in the bleak private waiting room, he was all at once out of control. Using a voice I'd never heard before.

"You're killing yourself! Don't you see, we've got

to give the jury something! You have to take the stand—don't you understand how it looks if you don't?"

"Yes," I said steadily enough. "It looks like I killed her."

For an instant I thought he might kill *me*, and I wished he would. But my father mauls only with words.

"Aren't you scared?" he said. "You should be." And he described prison to me; described in detail; described for a very, very long time.

Oh, yes, I was scared. I was being tried as an adult. Anyone would have been scared.

Especially after listening to Greg.

"Emily didn't dare tell anyone," Greg had explained rapidly on the stand to the prosecutor. To the jury. To his parents, who had published a vicious open letter to me in the newspaper. To everyone. "She was scared of Davey. But Emily couldn't keep her secret from me." His face was fevered. "Emily and I were very close," he said.

"It's my fault," Greg sobbed. "I thought if I were with her when she broke up with him, she'd be safe. I thought I could protect her. I should have listened to her when she told me he was out of control."

One woman on the jury reached out involuntarily, as if to pat Greg. But the others looked at me. Eleven pairs of eyes. Curious eyes. Judging eyes.

I had intended to stay silent. To keep off the stand. To let whatever happened to me happen. I had thought it all out very carefully, you see. I put all Greg's lies on one side of a scale, and I put the one truth on the other. And it seemed to me that it didn't matter that Greg had lied. Emily was dead.

By my hand.

But then I looked back at the jury. Even though Emily was dead, I looked back. I don't know why I had to, but I did. I met every pair of eyes.

Defend yourself, screamed my father. And in the end, out of fear, out of some blind need for survival, out of the vestiges of rage against Greg—for it was him I'd meant to hit, and both Greg and I knew it—I did.

I defended myself. I did it well, because Davey did everything well. And the facts, those the court considered important, were with me. There were no old bruises on Emily. The judge declared that Greg's history of drug abuse was admissible, and the jury looked at him differently after that. Then there were the bank statements for Greg and Emily's joint account, now empty. And the bank clerk who remembered Greg. "Oh, every week, he came," she said in her soft voice. "Then twice a week . . ."

The faces of the jurors changed. The shrieks of the tabloids softened, then died, then turned, snarling, on Greg. By the time the verdict came down, no one even seemed surprised.

No one but me.

Again I pictured Lily. I wondered what the jury would have thought if they had seen me with my eleven-year-old cousin that afternoon. If they had seen my upraised hand.

But I had *not* hit Lily. I had *not.* I held on to that as I lay in bed with my forearm over my open eyes. I had *not* done it. Not this time. And yet . . .

I recalled the strange expression on Lily's face. Suddenly I recognized it. I had seen it on Greg's face, when Emily fell. Before he buried it in the basement of his house of lies. It was . . .

Complicity.

CHAPTER 12

The next day exhaustion pressed on me like concrete. Only part of that day felt real: last period, in Dr. Walpole's class. There, I got a second wind and was able to sit up and pay attention of a kind.

Despite myself, I had become interested in the class. Up to then, we had been occupied by a rapid overview of the thousand-year period. Dr. Walpole was a good teacher: knowledgeable, and even, in her own dry way, dramatic. I would never forget her slides of the Kriminalmuseum in Rothenburg, with its elaborate instruments of torture. Who had ever heard of a punishment flute for bad musicians? Or a heavy metal mask with a tongue guard for gossips? Not to mention the more elaborate and horrible devices: racks, eye gougers, the inner-spiked case of an iron maiden. "Forget about criminals, witches, and heretics for a minute, people," said Dr. Walpole, "and notice how many of these instruments were used for day-to-day social control."

I wondered, with a kind of sick fascination, what they would have used on me. Or on Greg.

That day we were to announce our medieval identities: the point of view from which, said Dr. Walpole, we would individually grapple with the entire period. "And about which," she'd added, "you will write a major paper in the spring. So be careful. The character you pick—who can be real or imaginary—will be with you all year. Remember that if you choose to invent someone, you will still be responsible for collecting the background to form a realistic environment and opinions for your character."

In other words, it would be tougher to make someone up than to choose someone about whom you could just do specific research. I took the hint and chose a real person: Maimonides, a twelfth-century rabbinical scholar, philosopher, and physician. There was lots of material available about him, much of which was easily accessible via the Net.

I was the first person in the class to declare my choice. Dr. Walpole considered me over her half glasses and then nodded. "A fine choice." She wrote it down, and then said, "Stoph?"

While Christoph Khouri explained his choice (an elaborate imaginary identity for an eleventh-century fighting knight), I heard Frank Delgado whisper at me: "Hey."

This was unusual. Though we still sat side by side in Dr. Walpole's class, we had comprehensively ignored each other since he'd matter-of-factly identified the depth of my daily fear. I glanced over at him. "What?"

Frank replied, "I like Maimonides. I can see that his rationalism would appeal to you."

I blinked. I didn't quite know how to react. But it didn't matter; Frank had already half turned away to look toward Dr. Walpole, who was in the process of rejecting Justine Sinclair's choice. "I don't believe you've really considered the wide range of possibilities, Justine," she was saying.

"But I have, Dr. Walpole," said Justine earnestly. "Joan of Arc is a major figure. Don't you think she's fascinating?"

"I think everyone at this school already knows Joan's story," said Dr. Walpole. "Including you. Her presence will not add new information to our discussions; nor will you be challenged in the research phase." She paused. "How about Margery Kempe? She saw visions too." At that, I saw Frank smile to himself; clearly, he knew who this Margery Kempe was. I wanted to kick him.

Frank Delgado was last. I was curious about what identity he'd choose. It was almost certain to be someone we hadn't encountered in the background reading.

It was. "Abulafia," Frank said. His voice was very soft, close to inaudible. Oddly, he glanced over at me.

"I don't quite recall this Abulafia," said Dr. Walpole. It did not appear to disturb her. "Why don't you tell us a bit about this . . . it is a man, isn't it? A real person?"

"Yes," said Frank. "He was a kabbalist."

"Well, that helps," muttered Stoph Khouri.

"Kabbalism," Dr. Walpole said. "We didn't cover that material. Jewish medieval mysticism, yes?"

Frank nodded. "Kabbalists were mystics, yeah. They believed in all kinds of weird stuff. Magic. Astrology. Witches and demons. All the unexplainable stuff that medieval Christians believed in, but that most Jews, rational Jews like Maimonides"—again I got a glance—"didn't. The other Jews thought the kabbalists were crazy. And Abulafia—they thought he was the craziest one of all."

There was a little silence. Then, unexpectedly, Justine Sinclair said, "Oh, I see. Kind of like a medieval Fox Mulder." She added helpfully to Dr. Walpole, "*The X-Files*. On TV. Mulder and Scully investigate psychic phenomena. Mulder believes. Scully doesn't. She's the rational one."

Without thinking, I corrected her: "No, it's more complicated than that. Mulder *needs* to believe. His whole identity depends on it; it's what keeps him sane. It's a little twisted, but very logical."

Frank turned to look at me intently. Justine scowled. "Well, when you compare him to Scully, Mulder is *not* rational—"

I couldn't help myself. "Yes, he is! You just don't understand where he's coming from—" I stopped. Everyone was looking at me. Dr. Walpole opened her mouth.

Frank cut her off. "Yes?" he said to me.

I came to my senses. I slouched down in my chair. "Nothing," I said. "Off topic."

Dr. Walpole looked relieved. She nodded at Frank, who, astonishingly, had his mouth open again. "Fine,

70

then, Mr. Delgado," she said briskly. "You'll research this Abulafia." And she moved on, explaining how she expected our research to be conducted.

I felt Frank's curious eyes flick my way several times during the remainder of that class. I ignored him. I felt a little self-conscious, which was ridiculous.

The fact was that in a minor way I was an X-Phile. A fanatic. I had tapes of every episode. Avidly I followed all the discussions on the Net.

There was no reason to feel self-conscious about it. I was no different from hundreds—maybe thousands— of other fans. It was relaxing to go online and discuss the show anonymously. To spend hours dissecting its logical threads. To admire the courageous, analytical Scully. And, with Scully, to follow "Spooky" Mulder along his erratic, pain-filled path toward some elusive Truth that—you knew in your heart—would never restore his innocence even if he did find it.

CHAPTER 13

By the time I got home I felt terrible again. The mail didn't improve matters. It held a packet called "E-Apply!" which I had actually sent for, by clicking a button somewhere up in cyberspace. I opened the packet, and the names of umpteen hundred different colleges and universities danced dizzily down the information page. At the top a header screamed: "Do it electronically! Cut and paste your essays! Fast, convenient!" A CD-ROM tumbled out and I barely caught it. I leaned my shoulder up against the house for a minute.

My father had said that college applications were only permitted to ask if the applicant had ever been *convicted* of a felony. But it didn't matter; the admissions offices would remember me. They watched high schools for a living, didn't they? They'd have followed the case as a matter of professional interest.

"Hey. You okay?"

There was a tall girl standing next to me, frowning at me solicitously. I hadn't even heard her mount the porch steps. She had loose brown hair. She wore a man's white dress shirt open over a tight T-shirt. Baggy old jeans. Boots. Lipstick. Impartially speaking, and even in my current state, she was enough to make your mouth go dry.

Raina Doumeng. The artist who lived on the first floor; the one with the empty living room.

Somehow I managed to straighten up, and in the process I dropped the CD again. Raina caught it one-handed; looked at it. "Oh, yeah," she said. "What a nightmare. No wonder you look sick." She smiled and put out her hand, introduced herself. "I feel for you, really I do. I did all that two years ago. I'm at Tufts now, their joint program with the museum school." She said it like I was supposed to know what museum she meant.

"David," I said. I didn't include my last name. I couldn't, just then. She was so beautiful and she was smiling. "I live upstairs." We shook hands. Hers was callused. I fumbled for something else to say. I didn't want her to go in, to go away. I didn't want to be alone, even though it was better that way. "Uh—why don't you live on campus?"

"Oh, I need room. To paint, for one thing. Plus, I like privacy." She was examining my face, feature by feature. I knew she knew. I knew she was thinking about Emily. Thinking: *This is a killer.*

She said: "Hey, you got a Star Market card?"

73

"What?" I pulled myself together. "Uh, yeah." I did have a grocery card. You used it at the checkout and got discounts.

Raina extracted a blue card from her wallet. She held it out and, confused, I took it. ALAN BAWDEN, said the name on the card. She looked at me expectantly. "Well?" she said. "Give me yours."

My card said DAVID YAFFE. Uncertainly, I handed it over.

"Unbelievable. This one's really yours!" She shook her head. "Listen, start swapping, okay? The marketing people use these things to track our spending patterns. But if you swap, you thwart 'em. I trade at least once a week."

She seemed entirely earnest. She had already pocketed my card. I had a fleeting moment of suspicion . . . but what would the tabloids want with my supermarket card? "How do you trade?" I asked. "Do you just walk up to strangers and ask them?"

"Yeah." She smiled. "Like I just did."

Slowly, I put the ALAN BAWDEN card away. I was unable to find anything else to say. I looked at her. She looked back at me.

And then she seemed to come to some decision. "Want to come in for some tea? I'll tell you how to get through the college application stuff. You'll benefit from my mistakes."

I didn't think I would, but that hardly mattered. I couldn't understand why any girl would invite me anywhere. Any *sane* girl, that is. Maybe she really didn't recognize me; maybe that careful examination of my face was just the kind of thing artists did. I opened my mouth to say no. "Yeah," I said. "Okay."

I'd been wrong; her living room was not completely empty. There was simply no *furniture* in it. Instead, the two main walls were occupied by large canvases on which paintings—huge, colorful faces—were in progress. One short and one tall stepladder stood open in the middle of the room. The dining room was in exactly the same state, except it held three paintings and no ladders. The faces in the paintings were all different and yet they were not.

I stopped to look for a long time at one of them, a woman with calm opaque eyes and gaunt green cheeks.

"Do you just paint portraits?" I asked finally.

"Except for school assignments, yes. I'm obsessed with faces." My own face burned at that comment. Raina nodded toward the portrait at which I'd been staring. "That's my best friend's mother. Her name's Georgia."

I couldn't stop myself. I said, "She's very sick, isn't she?"

"Yes," said Raina. She sounded surprised.

"It's a good picture," I said. I looked away from it, and the others. I met Raina's eyes for an instant, until hers flicked away. I knew with deep certainty, then, that she did recognize me. *I'm obsessed with faces.* And I knew why she had invited me in.

"I promised you tea," said Raina. "And college advice. Come on."

I should leave now, I thought. I could feel the portrait watching me. I wondered how that woman felt about being painted with her fate naked in her eyes.

I wondered why people—Raina, that photographer

75

who shot the picture of my parents—wanted to capture such things. I wondered why people wanted to look at them. Did it make them feel safer somehow? Removed? Did it make them feel they could see the other side of the abyss that separated people like them from people like me? Did they *want* to see it?

Or did they not understand what they were seeing at all?

I followed Raina into the kitchen. There was some furniture there: a scuffed folding table and two mismatched chairs.

"That chair's not so steady," said Raina. She was running sink water into a couple of mugs, which she placed in the microwave. "Try the other one." The oven roared into tinny operation. "Do you take milk in your tea?"

I didn't know. I never drank tea. "Black's fine," I said.

She went rummaging in the refrigerator anyway, and emerged bearing a quart of milk and a plastic lemon. She tossed the lemon at me underhand. She sniffed the milk and then poured it down the sink. "Go on, sit down," she said.

I sat.

The microwave beeped. Raina grabbed the mugs and plunked them down on the table. A second later she had teabags floating in them. She sat down on the rickety chair and looked at me while stirring her tea idly with a fingertip. Apparently her household goods did not extend to spoons. "So, right. College," she said. "I guess my advice is to remember that it's not as important as they make it seem. If you listen to other people, you'd think it's all over if you make the wrong move. Well, it's not—"

"Please stop it," I said quietly. It just came out. I wasn't angry at her for the stupid college talk. I just wanted her—wanted someone—to be honest.

Silence. Finally I looked up. Raina was watching me calmly, curiously. I thought I should go. I wanted to go. And I didn't. I looked at my tea. I sipped it. It tasted horrible. "You know who I am," I said. "You invited me in because you want to paint me. Right? Just say it. It's okay. I just—I can't stand the small talk."

Raina still didn't say anything. She picked up her mug. She sipped it and watched me, and oddly, it wasn't so uncomfortable, not once I had spoken my mind.

Then she said, "David Bernard Yaffe."

My family never used my middle name, but the newspapers did. "Yeah," I said.

She said, quietly, "Since you bring it up, do you want me to paint you?"

"No!"

She looked at me with those eyes that saw death in her best friend's mother and painted it so anyone could see. "That's that, then," she said calmly. "Let me know if you change your mind. More tea?"

She smiled, and reluctantly I noticed again how beautiful she was. Not like Emily. No one was Emily, or ever again would be. But still beautiful.

It was in my mind and I couldn't help myself. My mouth opened. I blurted out: "Aren't you afraid of me? Don't you think I'm probably some monster?"

Raina smiled a little, as if I were far younger than I

77

was. "No. Not at all. It was pretty clear what had happened, by the end. Don't you think?"

I looked away from her. Was she blind? Stupid? Were they all?

She said, "More tea?"

I said, "Yes. Okay."

No one feared me—except me.

I so much wanted to believe them.

CHAPTER 14

Unless you counted that weird challenge from Frank Delgado, Raina Doumeng was the first new person I'd met with whom I'd had anything approaching a truthful conversation. I was conscious of that, even as we moved on to innocuous subjects. And later, when I mentioned Dr. Walpole's medieval history seminar, she invited me to go to a museum with her on Saturday, to look at medieval art.

Not a date, I told myself. Just a museum. "Okay," I said.

"Excellent," said Raina casually. "You'll like this stuff."

Saying good-bye to her, going upstairs to the attic, I felt better than usual. That night and for the next few nights, I even slept fairly well, undisturbed by—or perhaps simply used to—the humming shadow. Even Lily's knowing glance, directed at me whenever I ran into her over the remainder of that week, could not spoil my mood.

I was amused to notice that Raina had been right about the supermarket card swapping. Once I knew to look for it, I saw it all over the city. A cute girl silently swapped with a guy at a bus stop, and then turned and walked away, swaying flirtatiously. Inside a convenience store, two harassed mothers traded almost absently, by the dairy case: "Swap?" "Sure." All you needed to do, it seemed, was take out a supermarket card in any public place and dangle it. Within a few days I had swapped ALAN BAWDEN for AMY CONKLIN and then for SUZANNE WERTHEIM. This last swap occurred right at the supermarket checkout; the clerk grabbed my card for scanning and switched it with another so rapidly that I almost missed it. I did, however, catch the barest smile on her lips.

Friday was my eighteenth birthday. It passed uneventfully, the occasion marked only by a phone call from my mother and the arrival of a massive check from my father. I was relieved that Vic and Julia didn't know, or had forgotten, the date. I wanted it to be over as quickly as possible.

On the next day, Saturday, I woke up early and went for a long run through North Cambridge and around Fresh Pond. I was supposed to meet Raina in Harvard Square at noon, in front of the Fogg Museum. "I have to work in the morning," she'd said. "So let's just meet there."

I wondered where she worked. I wondered if she could possibly be a friend. She was so beautiful. If things were different . . .

But they weren't.

The fact that Raina and I were meeting in Harvard Square instead of at the house we both lived in gave the outing a clandestine feel. But I was also relieved. For some reason I didn't want to conduct this . . . *friendship* with Raina in view of my relatives. Particularly I did not want to expose it to Lily.

Lily the minefield.

On the way back upstairs after my run, Vic called my name, so I had to stick my head in the kitchen door. Vic and Lily were at the table with identical bowls of cereal; Lily's head was bent low over hers as, ignoring me, she carefully drowned individual Froot Loops in milk. Julia stood by the counter with a cup of coffee and the sales circulars; her lips pursed sourly at my greeting. Her eyes were alert.

She barely waited for Vic to finish speaking. "About Thanksgiving," Julia said. "Tell your mother that *I* will roast the turkey. And we'll eat down here. You haven't enough room for all of us. And also . . ." She had four or five other things, ticked off on her fingers, that I was to communicate to my mother.

"Sure, I can tell her," I finally interrupted. "But maybe it would be better if you just called her yourself to make plans? I might not remember everything."

Julia opened her mouth again, but I cut her off with an ostentatious glance at my watch. "Gotta run," I said, which was true. "See you later." And I pounded on up the stairs, relieved that at least Lily had had nothing to say. She hadn't actually said a word to me since our encounter over the rakes, and I was glad. It was odd, though. Lily's personality, which I felt so

81

strongly when I was alone with her, seemed to disappear in the presence of her parents.

I took the subway to Harvard Square and got to the museum ten minutes late. Raina was sitting on the steps outside, wearing clothes nearly identical to those she'd had on earlier in the week.

"Sorry," I puffed. I followed Raina as she picked up a floor plan of the museum and then decisively led me into the first of several rooms containing medieval art. There were triptychs and icons and panels, mostly of saints and martyrs, all very colorful and rather flat in appearance. She stopped right in the center of the room. "I love this stuff," she said. She nodded toward a triptych that was brilliant in reds and blues and golds, and we went closer.

The center panel depicted a beautiful, skinny man bleeding luridly from the wounds of a dozen arrows. He was wearing a sheer white cloth around his loins, a lofty, almost silly expression, and a deep golden halo that sat behind and on top of his head like a paper circle. On the left and right panels a richly dressed man and a woman knelt in prayerful profile.

"St. Sebastian," Raina said with satisfaction. "You can always tell by the arrows." She gestured at the profiled couple. "Bet these folks commissioned the piece as insurance against plague. That's Sebastian's job."

"Excuse me?" I said.

"There's a saint for everything," explained Raina. "You can pray to St. Apollonia to cure a toothache, or to St. Blaise when you've got a sore throat." She paused. "Maybe, today, people pray to St. Sebastian for protection against HIV."

I watched the side of her face. "You Catholic?" I asked.

Raina shrugged. "No. I'm not anything."

I don't know why I asked. But I did. "Do you believe in God?"

Raina turned and looked me full in the eyes. "Yes. Absolutely."

I was surprised. Almost shocked. I don't know why. Raina asked, "What about you?"

"No," I said. My voice came out a little too loud for a museum. I lowered it. "I just don't," I said. Why had I brought this up? Thankfully, Raina did not pursue the subject.

We moved from room to room together, casual. It was comfortable. I liked her. But whenever we were quiet, I kept thinking of Emily. It had been foolish to imagine, even for a moment, that I might not.

CHAPTER 15

Thanksgiving morning. I opened one eye at a rustling in the kitchen, and then closed it quickly, turning over on the sofa to present my mother—should she look at me—with my back. Surreptitiously, I maneuvered my wrist into position and peeked at my watch. Six A.M.

My sofa was not long enough to accommodate six-footers, and I had slept uneasily, too aware of my parents' presence. They had arrived fairly late the night before, tired from the trip, and had tumbled almost immediately into bed in my room. Vic had offered me the pullout sofabed downstairs in their apartment, but the last thing I wanted was to wake up in the Shaughnessy living room. I didn't want to be so near Lily. For the last couple of weeks, she'd been watching my arrivals and departures like a sharpshooter, making me very nervous as well as superconscious of the few times Raina treated me to tepid tea. I wondered if either my mother or my father would notice the too sharp way Lily sometimes eyed me.

Or maybe they'd be too busy eyeing me themselves to notice.

No sooner had I had the thought than my mother spoke. "David? Are you awake?"

I was about to emit an artistic little snore, but abruptly decided it wasn't worth it. I sat up slowly. "Yeah. I guess." I inhaled deeply: orange rind, lemon rind, and sherry. Also coffee.

"Good," she said. "In a little while, I'll need some help getting the bird down the stairs and into Julia's oven. Your father's still asleep."

I nodded, and my mother smiled at me over the kitchen counter. I made a similar facial motion and broke eye contact, feeling awkward.

My mother had of course won her battle with Julia to prepare the turkey. One of her hands was holding a twenty-five-pound bird steady; the other was spooning in stuffing. Ingredients for the stuffing littered the counter. A large brown paper bag waited to encase the turkey during roasting.

I had not been looking forward to this, but now, smelling the citrus and sherry, seeing the familiar paper bag, I could almost feel things were normal. I caught my mother's eye—it wasn't difficult, she was watching me closely while pretending not to—and I said, "That smells great."

I got up, stretched, and squeezed past her in the kitchen in one direction to get to the cereal, and then in the other to the coffee. I ate in silence while my mother finished preparing the turkey. "If we get this in

85

by seven," she said, "it'll come out around one-thirty, and we'll be ready to carve a little while after."

"Sounds good," I said. I wondered if Vic would want to watch football. My father would. I wanted to. It was something my father and I could do without needing to talk. "When's . . ." My tongue stumbled a little but then I recovered. "When's Dad getting up?"

"In a couple hours, maybe. Yesterday's drive tired him out."

Reprieved, I nodded. I finished my cereal and drank a second cup of coffee. Then I helped my mother tuck the turkey into the paper bag in the roasting pan. "Are you sure the bag won't catch fire?" I teased, as I always had, and my mother shook her head at me indulgently.

"It keeps the turkey moist," she said, smiling. "Without basting." She accompanied me downstairs and supervised the insertion of the bird into Julia's oven. Julia and Vic were not up, but Lily was.

Lily wore a faded pink flannel nightgown, and her feet were bare. She murmured a greeting in response to my mother's, but sneered at me. I turned my back on her, and then, to look like I'd had a reason for turning away, I fingered the controls of the oven.

"David! Don't mess with the temperature," said my mother, alarmed. She turned toward Lily. "Lily, dear, would you like to come upstairs with David and me and have some cereal? Or scrambled eggs? I make wonderful eggs."

"I don't have any eggs in the fridge," I said. I'd meant it only as a point of information, but my mother shot me a look, and so—with a secret smile beginning to curve her lips—did Lily.

"That would be very nice, Aunt Eileen," said Lily then, her tone almost chirpy. "I like scrambled eggs. And you could use some of my mother's eggs. She gets them from a farm stand."

"Wonderful," said my mother. Her back informed me that I was persona non grata. I trailed her, Lily, and a carton of eggs back upstairs.

By halfway through the morning, I had a severe headache. Lily had spent a solid two hours with my mother, during which she'd explained in detail why ice-skater Tara Lipinski was her favorite. She'd eaten two scrambled eggs with cheese and asked, shyly, for a third. She'd described a skating exhibition Vic had taken her to the previous winter; who had skated, what costumes they'd worn and what music they'd used. She had not, in short, shut up.

It was a Lily I'd never seen before: a normal, cheery eleven-year-old. Throughout, she called my mother Aunt Eileen just a little too often—"Aunt Eileen? She was wearing this dress, with, you know, Aunt Eileen, silver and pearl all around the neck. Really pretty, Aunt Eileen!" And, occasionally, she would cast a sidelong, triumphant glance at me as I slouched on the sofa pretending to read college catalogs. Somehow, between the Aunt Eileens and the sneaky looks, I got the idea that this performance was aimed at me.

Beyond that, of course, I was waiting for my father to get up. Not looking at the bedroom door. But alert. Tense. Waiting.

Finally, around ten o'clock, he came stumbling out of the bedroom in his robe. I felt a little shock: he didn't look so formidable. He kissed my mother and looked at me, and I looked back. His hair had more gray in it than I had remembered. Or maybe you could just see the gray more easily when it was rumpled.

"Good morning," he said.

"Good morning," I said. He had touched my shoulder briefly the night before, when they arrived. I could still feel it. He did nothing now. But we had never been a touchy-feely family.

After a minute my father said, "I smell coffee," and I relaxed. And, thankfully, Lily toned herself down. She regarded my father warily and, after a few minutes, retreated downstairs with my mother, who wanted to check her turkey.

This left me alone with my father. We read the newspaper. I took a couple of aspirin. Then my mother called upstairs for us to join them.

"Here goes nothing," muttered my father. Startled, I looked at him. "It's Julia," he said. "She's always scared me." He half smiled, and shrugged toward my TV. "Can we sneak up here and catch the game later?"

"Yeah," I said cautiously.

Downstairs the smell of the turkey had begun to fill the house. In the living room, my mother was talking to Julia and Vic. I couldn't help noticing Julia's and Vic's relative positions, each isolated in chairs on opposite sides of the room. Lily sat near my mother on the sofa, her eyes unfocused, daydreaming. My father took a chair near Vic. I sat down on the other side of my mother and followed Lily's example of silence. I wondered where Raina was spending her Thanksgiving.

". . . all settled in?"

I became aware of expectant glances. In my head, I rewound the last few noises I'd heard and replayed them, searching for meaning. "Uh, yeah," I ventured. "I guess so."

"At school, too?" It was Julia speaking, her head cocked to one side, her posture straight as a floor lamp, her tone polite but insistent.

"Yeah," I said. Julia still looked expectant, so I tried to think of something to add, but failed.

"Vic and I," said Julia to my mother, "have tried to make David as comfortable as possible here, but he hasn't been very forthcoming about his life."

I suppressed a snort. Even if I had felt inclined to confide in Julia, I had seen her perhaps three times since she'd invited me to dinner back in September. And Julia's coy "Vic and I"—well, even Lily would find that funny. But when I turned my head toward her to check, she was watching her mother with her fists clenched in her lap and her jaw tight.

Okay, so maybe Julia wasn't funny.

Across the room from Julia, Vic fidgeted. He spoke also to my mother. "I'm sure David would tell us if something were wrong."

"I'm sure," said my mother.

"New schools take getting used to," said my father, unexpectedly.

"Very true," said my mother.

A silence—that special Shaughnessy silence—fell, and lasted. Vic huddled in his Barcalounger. Julia and my mother kept smiles pasted on their mouths. My father's glasses slipped down the bridge of his nose, indicating disengagement. Lily watched all of us, her head moving like a bird's as her gaze darted from face to face.

My mother commanded me with her eyes: *Help!* I shook my head, and she nodded hers as vehemently as possible given that she was trying to be discreet. I knew I ought to help with the conversation, but my mind was blank. This was even more difficult than I had imagined.

Vic said something, but his voice was too low to hear.

"Vic?" asked my mother. "Did you want to say—"

Simultaneously, Julia's voice cut across my mother's. "Lily," she said. "Tell your father to speak up so that we—" She stopped, but it was too late. Lily grinned. Triumphantly.

"Mom says you should speak up, Dad," said Lily to her father. "So that people can hear you."

Julia opened her mouth again, but nothing came out. Her throat moved as she swallowed, and, beneath my embarrassment and horror, I felt a sudden empathy for her; after all, this was her home, her life, and she hadn't wanted any of us in it. Then, as if she'd had this thought too, Julia raised her chin, her face defiant, proud. Waiting for the in-laws she didn't like to judge her and her marriage.

Vic, meanwhile, had his eyes fixed on my mother's face. "Eileen. Eileen, I . . . we—"

"Dad," Lily interrupted, "don't worry. I'm sure Aunt Eileen can understand that I always talk to you for Mom, and to Mom for you. Right, Aunt Eileen?" She was feeling confident enough even to address my father, who, a minute before, had pushed his glasses up to sit squarely in front of his eyes and was regarding Lily steadily through them. "Uncle Stuart?"

"Yes." My mother swallowed. "Of course we understand."

"Good," said Lily. She smiled at Vic, and then at Julia. "See, there's nothing to worry about."

Vic looked sick.

Julia's lips pursed. She said nothing.

I didn't have to look at my mother to feel her desperation. "There's a skinhead in one of my classes at St. Joan's," I said. "What do you think of that?" I was immediately sorry, wishing I'd said something else—anything else. But it was too late. Everyone turned toward me, even Lily, and there was a relieved babble of curious voices. Julia's won.

"A skinhead?" she said. "I read something in the paper about that. At a public school, nearby. I forget where. Apparently there are lots of these neo-Nazi kids around. Well, there must be, if they're at St. Joan's."

"They do say these groups are growing," said my mother. "Scary." She frowned at me. "So, this boy—"

"Uh, I'm not sure he's that kind of skinhead," I said, suddenly seeing Frank Delgado's face in my mind and feeling guilty. "You know, a neo-Nazi. I think he just—"

But Lily's voice cut right across mine. "A neo-Nazi?" she said perkily. "I know about them." She turned to me. "So, does this boy in your class want to kill you? Because you're Jewish?"

For a moment, no one spoke. From behind his glasses, my father's eyes caught mine, frowning, curi-

91

ous. I looked away. Then Vic and Julia and my mother all began talking at once, and this time, my mother's voice overrode the others.

"Come with me to the kitchen, Lily," she said. "I want to check on the turkey."

"But I—"

"We'll talk in the kitchen."

They left. After a couple of seconds, my father said to me quietly, "Lily doesn't like you, David."

I looked at him, forgetting—as he surely had—that Vic and Julia were in the room. For a second, we were back in the courthouse. He was screaming at me. He'd thought he could lawyer everything right.

He was watching me now—*judging*—like he'd watched me then.

It was more complicated than dislike. Lily wanted something from me; was purposely trying to goad me. And though I didn't know what Lily wanted—didn't know what was hidden beneath her intensity and her oddness—I also knew I didn't *want* to know. I had my own problems.

I thought of that portrait in Raina's living room, of the woman with the abyss in her eyes, and I put on my best blank face. "I'm not sure—" I began.

Julia saved me. "That's a remarkable conclusion to draw, Stuart," she said crisply. "Aren't you being a little melodramatic?"

"I agree with Julia," said Vic. "Lily likes you perfectly well, David. She's a little excited today, maybe, but for Stuart to leap to the conclusion that she doesn't like you, well, that's—"

"Melodramatic, as Julia says," said my father equably. "I apologize. Let's forget it." He nodded at Vic and Julia, but he didn't look at me. Anyway, he was using his courtroom voice, his reasonable voice. He had not changed his mind.

He's acute, my father. Just not acute enough.

Vic relaxed. "Lily was just interested," he said. "Like Julia said, that kind of thing . . ." His voice faltered for a moment. "You know, skinheads and such, they've been in the local news."

"In Everett," added Julia.

"Uh-huh," said my father.

Vic was frowning. "I can't remember exactly what it was about."

"A cemetery," said Julia. "Three boys desecrated a cemetery."

"Yes," said Vic. "That's it. It even looked like a teacher was involved."

"They couldn't prove that, Victor," corrected Julia. "There was no evidence—" She stopped. She stared at her husband, and he stared back, both evidently realizing the same thing that I had just understood: They had been conversing directly. Without Lily.

"There was no hard evidence that the teacher was involved," finished Vic. He hesitated, and then looked directly at Julia. "You're right about that," he said. "Julia."

At first I thought Julia was not going to reply. She turned away from Vic and opened her mouth as if to speak to my father. Then, slowly, her head swiveled back. "Thank you," she said. "Victor."

Involuntarily, I looked at my father. He shook his head incredulously. We watched as Victor and Julia looked at each other for a long time.

Then, in the doorway, I noticed Lily. I could tell from her expression that she had witnessed what had just happened between her parents. But I would have needed to stand for hours before a painting of Lily by Raina Doumeng before I would have been able to see what she felt about it.

Except—it was not joy.

CHAPTER 16

Over the Thanksgiving meal, Vic and Julia continued to speak to each other. Their comments, uttered with a certain self-consciousness, were entirely trivial: "Pass the salt, please, Victor," and "Delicious rice pilaf, Julia." But they came regularly, almost doggedly, and each one was accompanied by a name as if, like a letter without an address, it would otherwise go astray. Seeing and hearing their exchange was painful. I kept my eyes averted from their faces and ate. I ate a lot, to keep my mouth obviously occupied.

As Julia complimented Vic on his turkey carving, I wondered if it was all a sham staged for my parents' benefit. But Lily didn't think so. She sat tensely at the table, her head lifting a fraction if one of her parents spoke. When Julia asked for the salt, Lily reached for it. And then she snatched her hand back as Julia pronounced her husband's name.

I'd have felt sympathy for Lily, but just then she elbowed the butter dish into my lap, and I'd swear it was deliberate.

Before this, I'd dreaded spending time alone with my father. But after a couple of hours with the Shaughnessys I was relieved when the meal ended. My mother stayed downstairs talking with Lily, but my father and I went upstairs and watched football in almost complete silence. And it was okay.

After the game, we went back downstairs, and my mother suggested a stroll outside. I thought at first she meant only my father, but she turned to me and said, "Coming, David?" She even made a little face, jerking her chin marginally toward Vic and Julia, who were seated stiffly together on the sofa.

"Okay," I said.

"Lily?" said my mother. "Will you show us around the neighborhood?"

"No," said Lily flatly.

"But we really would love you to come," said my mother.

"I want to stay here," said Lily. She did not look at her parents.

"But—" said my mother.

"Eileen," said my father quietly. "It's Lily's decision."

My mother sighed. "Well, Lily. Feel free to come and catch up with us if you change your mind." But before she was half through with her sentence, Lily had turned her back and gone to sit on the sofa. Between her parents.

"Let's go," said my father. We started downstairs.

"Stuart," said my mother softly.

"Not here, Eileen."

I feared I would be asked about Lily. I dreaded it. I prayed suddenly, intensely, for a distraction, and I got one. Raina Doumeng was on the porch.

"Well, hello," she said. She had a huge, soft-looking black shawl wrapped around her, a portfolio under her arm, and an uncertain smile on her face. She looked at my parents curiously.

"Hey, Raina," I said, a little nervously. "Meet my parents." I performed introductions. I even remembered to say "Museum school" about Raina.

"How impressive! The Museum of Fine Arts program doesn't take many undergraduates," said my mother, who knows everything. "And how long have you been living here?" She gestured at the front door of Raina's apartment.

"A little over a year," said Raina, shifting on the heels of her boots. Failing to notice that my mother had begun another polite comment, she said, "David. I have something for you." She began fumbling with the ties of her portfolio; her shawl slipped unnoticed down her shoulders to hang in the crooks of her elbows.

"Maybe later," I said. My mother was watching Raina with what I felt was undue interest.

Raina didn't look up. "Later I might have lost it." She had the portfolio open, and was sorting quickly through the contents. She located a newspaper clipping, and held it out to me.

I took the clipping. It was a review of an art exhibit at M.I.T. "Anxious Salon: The Naked and the Dread," read the headline.

"Thanks," I said. Raina looked expectant, so I began scanning the text.

"No, no," said Raina impatiently. She stepped next to me and leaned in, pointing. She seemed to have completely forgotten that my parents were there. "Look at the *picture*."

It was a detail from a painting, showing a nude, muscled young man in an ass-head mask. Around his neck was a necklace of thorns, with a swastika hanging from it. His head was completely bald.

I thought, *I shouldn't have talked to* her *about Frank Delgado either. Everyone's overreacting.* But I hadn't had much I *could* talk about. Frank had seemed a safe enough topic.

Raina's voice was surprisingly loud as she spoke to my parents. "David was telling me about the kid in his class with the shaved head, and then this exhibit pops up. There's quite a movement going on with this stuff in the art world . . ." She chattered on, responding to my mother's questions, my father's eyebrow. She didn't appear to notice my silence. I was furious at myself. Why had I mentioned Frank Delgado to Raina, in one of those silent pauses over tea? I did not want to make a big deal over him. He wasn't a neo-Nazi. He just had a shaved head. He was just a weird kid with a shaved head.

"The article's reproduction is pretty bad," Raina was saying to my parents. "Apparently the artist is getting to be well known . . . Yes, absolutely controversial . . . painted in Berlin . . . No, just because he paints this stuff doesn't mean he himself approves of it. But then again—well, I'd have to see the whole exhibit, read some critics . . . Yes, there's certainly something sexual, Mapplethorpeish about this one . . . Oh, yes, I'm sure David will want to see the exhibit—"

"No," I said. "I don't."

They all looked at me. "Well, fine," said Raina. "Then don't." I knew she was offended.

"David, are you sure?" my mother asked. "It's nearby, and I'd love to see it. We could go tomorrow."

"I thought we'd go for a hike in the Blue Hills," I said. "I hear there's a terrific view of Boston."

There was a pause.

"I'm not the hiking type, dear," said my mother dryly. Then her face brightened with an idea. "Stuart, you and David could go for that hike, while Raina and I—" She swiveled and looked at Raina. "You do want to see this exhibit? How about tomorrow? Are you busy?"

"Well . . . ," said Raina. She was looking a little flustered. "I hadn't planned . . . that is, I'd love to."

"Excellent," said my mother, beaming. "And perhaps you'd like to come upstairs for dinner afterward. I plan to cook salmon."

I could feel my father next to me. I imagined us alone together for hours and I panicked. "Changed my mind," I said. "I'll go to the exhibit too."

"All right," said my mother quietly, after a moment.

I did not look at my father. He did not look at me.

Raina said good-bye, and went inside. And we went for our walk. "A nice girl," said my mother about Raina, but thankfully she left it at that. We three walked through the North Cambridge streets for a full

99

hour, and spoke only about the neighborhood. It was what I had wanted. No questions about Lily, or Julia, or Vic, or Raina, or even about Frank Delgado.

As we neared the Shaughnessy house again, my father said, "Perhaps your mother and I will take another turn around the block."

"Okay," I said. I knew I had hurt him when I dodged the hike. I tried not to be hurt now. I left them. I went in alone.

Running up the inside stairs in the gloom, I nearly tripped over Lily. She was sitting on the top step outside her parents' apartment. Without looking at me, she squeezed her body to the left. I stepped by. If she was going to ignore me, then I would ignore her.

But then, about to nudge the door closed, I hesitated. "Lily? Aren't you coming in?" She didn't answer. I took a deep breath. "Aren't you cold?"

From deeper within the apartment, I heard Julia's laugh, and then Vic's. At the sound of their laughter, gooseflesh rose on my arms. It was so . . . so tentative. And it sounded so peculiar, in that house.

There was no laughter in that house. Only shadows, humming, and silence.

I looked at the back of Lily's neck, at the way she sat, upright, on the stair. I stood there for several minutes as the gooseflesh settled. Finally, I closed the door, leaving it unlocked behind me. Let Lily sit there if she wanted, if it helped. She'd get over it.

Surely she would get over it.

CHAPTER 17

My mother liked Raina. By the time the salmon dinner was eaten the following evening, it was clear to me that my mother liked Raina very much.

My father, as always, was harder to figure. I caught him watching me, and I knew that unlike my mother, he had not rushed into assuming Raina was a potential new girlfriend.

The four of us were in the attic apartment. My mother had invited Vic and Julia, and Lily, and had bought plenty of fish and vegetables, but Vic and Julia had other plans.

"There's a movie at the Capitol," said Julia, "which Vic and I have decided to see." She named a Meg Ryan romantic comedy. There was a faint pink tinge on her cheeks. My mother beamed at her. "Lily will come to dinner," said Julia.

But Lily had not come. And when I was sent down

to fetch her, I found a locked bedroom door and silence behind it. She didn't respond to me, or to my mother, or to my father, and finally we left her alone.

"She'll get over it," said my mother uncertainly as she cut lemon for the fish. My father had gone back downstairs to tell Lily we would put a plate for her in the kitchen. "And the salmon and asparagus will be fine cold."

I nodded. Then my father came back, with Raina, who had actually changed for dinner.

She wasn't ever going to be my girlfriend. That kind of thing was over for me. But even so, I could hardly breathe for a moment as I looked at her. She had on a short skirt and black tights covered with tiny white dots. She abandoned her shoes at the door when she came in, and sat down in a corner of the sofa, folding her long legs up under her. Her lipstick shimmered.

Her shirt was unfortunately very baggy.

I listened to her chatter unself-consciously with my parents: her classes, her three part-time jobs, her paintings, her hopes.

Soon I managed to forget Lily, alone downstairs, and things went very well until after dinner, when my mother pulled a little photo album out of her purse. Her sly, happy, sidelong glance toward me made me tighten in fear. I winced under the weight of the normalcy she wished me to reclaim.

I went to the kitchen, made coffee, and scooped out ice cream for everyone.

Raina flipped through the photos one by one as my mother provided the primary narration and my father, on my mother's other side, threw in the occasional comment. "These are great, Eileen," said Raina to my mother, about halfway through, and the name sounded so odd. Emily had always called my parents Mr. and Mrs. Yaffe.

"Here's David on the swings," said my mother happily, and I grimaced. I handed around the ice cream and coffee and leaned over the back of the sofa, where I had an excellent view of Raina's legs and a less-than-excellent view of the photographs.

"David's Little League team," said my father. "David is, uh—"

"Right there," said Raina, unerringly picking out the ten-year-old me in the lineup. I was impressed. Even I had had trouble locating myself in that one.

Raina turned the page. "Oh, look. There's a picture tucked behind this one." She pulled it out. I knew instantly who it was.

I said, "Kathy." And as I spoke her name I had a flash of déjà vu, as if I'd seen her recently. For the barest instant I heard the humming, and I froze. I looked around, but no one else appeared to have heard a thing. I pulled myself together.

"My cousin," I said to Raina. "Vic and Julia's older daughter." I was aware, again, of Lily downstairs. "Lily's sister."

"She looks a lot like you, Eileen," said Raina to my mother. "Where is she now?" But my mother was staring at the photo and didn't answer.

"She's dead," I said, and my voice was much too loud in the apartment that had been Kathy's.

"Oh!" Raina flushed. "I'm so sorry. How sad." She paused. "She can't have been very old."

"Eighteen." My mother took the photo. "I'm sorry," she said to Raina. "I was just surprised . . ." Then she turned to me. "I went through all the photos before coming, because you said there weren't any of Kathy downstairs. I must have missed it somehow." She exhaled. My father put his arm around her and she leaned against him. "Thank God this didn't happen in front of Vic and Julia. I can't imagine what I'd have done . . . especially now."

"It didn't happen," said my father.

"Yes, but what if—"

"It didn't happen." He smiled at her, and after a moment she smiled back gratefully.

I looked at the photo. Raina was right; Kathy did resemble my mother. I said so.

"It's the jaw," said Raina, the portrait painter. "And the nose, the brow; the underlying structure. It's only the coloring that's different." With a finger, she traced the lines of Kathy's face in the photograph. I followed her eyes to my mother's face and I could see what she meant.

"Can I keep this?" I said to my mother.

She frowned. "Well, if you want. Just don't let Julia—"

"I'll be careful," I said.

There was one of those pauses. "Well," said Raina, and I knew she was about to leave. Part of me wanted her to, immediately. That part of me resented the illusion her presence created—the illusion that I was okay, had a girlfriend, was back to normal. But the other part of me welcomed it.

Surprisingly, my father said, "Eileen, let's go downstairs and try again to talk to Lily."

"Oh, yes," said my mother.

And Raina didn't leave. Instead, she reached for her melting ice cream. "They're nice, your parents," she said after they'd gone.

"They like you," I said. I paused, embarrassed. "My mother seems to think . . ."

"Yeah. Don't worry about it," said Raina casually. She finished her ice cream and put the dish down. She stretched out her legs. I wanted to say something, but didn't know what. I was conscious of the cooling coffee, of the ice cream dishes. Of Raina's legs, and of her eyes examining me. I was glad when she spoke.

"I can't help being curious about your cousin Kathy. She died very young. How did it happen?"

Again I was aware that this had been Kathy's apartment. Raina added, "Of course you don't have to tell me if it's too painful or something."

"No," I said, "it's okay. It's just . . ." I cast around and seized upon a random excuse. "I should do the dishes."

"I'll help," said Raina. "You can tell me while we do them." We gathered everything up and transferred it to the sink. I washed and Raina dried. Her eyes were expectant, and I had no reason not to tell her. None.

"She was twelve years older than Lily," I said. "Lily was a big surprise—Kathy had been the only child for so long. Vic and Julia had all these plans for Kathy." I hesitated.

Raina dried the last dish and I let the water out of the sink. As it gurgled down the pipes, Raina said, straight out, "Kathy killed herself, didn't she?"

"Yeah," I said. I looked out at the living room. I felt cold. "She dropped out of college after her freshman year, and she lived here. Vic renovated this attic for her. She had a job, I think at a health club. She was learning to give aerobics classes, stuff like that. She had a boyfriend. I guess he dumped her. I don't know the details."

"Oh," said Raina. She, too, looked out at the living room. She said, "You must think about her a lot, living here."

"No," I said uncertainly. But my mind leapt unbidden to the humming shadow. I could almost see Kathy's twelve-year-old face, when I, at seven, had adored her. "I barely knew her."

"I would think about her," said Raina. "It's only natural."

I shrugged. I moved back to the living room and Raina followed me, close.

"How'd she do it?" she asked softly.

I turned to face her. "She took an overdose of something. That's all I know."

Raina wrapped her arms around herself as if she were suddenly cold. She started to say something and then stopped. Impulsively, I put a hand on her arm. "I'm sorry. You did ask. I didn't mean to upset you."

"It's okay," said Raina. She looked at me, her eyes and lips level with mine. My head swam. And then I thought of Emily. I stepped back.

Raina made a small gesture with her head. She moved her shoulders. She turned away, and then half turned back. "Um. When are your parents leaving?"

"Sunday."

"Well . . . you want to see a movie Sunday night?" Her eyes met mine straight on. "Like, um, a date?"

I wanted to say yes. I wanted so much to say yes. "I don't know," I said. "It's not you, it's . . . I . . . I'm sorry."

Raina reddened. "That's okay," she said. "Forget it."

I couldn't bear it. I didn't have anybody. I said, "Can we just go and see a movie, and not call it a date?"

For an excruciating moment I thought she would say no. But then she nodded, and I could breathe again. "Okay. An early movie, then?"

I nodded. Somehow I composed myself enough to add, "Can we see something really dumb?"

"No," said Raina firmly. She even smiled a little. "There're some short student art films at the museum."

I groaned, but it was just for show and we both knew that. "Okay."

We stood a bit awkwardly, listening to my parents' footsteps as they climbed the stairs. And then they came in, and Raina said good night and left.

"Any luck with Lily?" I said to my parents. I hoped to forestall any comments about Raina.

"Well," said my father, "eventually she opened the door a crack and said that we'd woken her up and she hated us. I don't think she really was sleeping, though. Her light was on the whole time. You could see it under the door." He took off his glasses and rubbed the bridge of his nose. "She'll need a good week of sulking, I'd guess. Maybe two. Then she'll snap out of it."

"Yeah," I said, but privately I doubted it.

My mother was looking at me. "David? I was wondering—why do you want Kathy's picture?"

"No reason," I said uncomfortably. "I just remember her." And then I said something that, until that moment, I had not realized I knew. "Kathy died *here*, didn't she?" I said. "Here, in this attic."

"Yes," said my father.

"She died here alone," I said. I felt as if a piece of a puzzle—a puzzle I hadn't known I was working on—had slotted into place. "All alone."

There was a little silence.

"Why, no," said my mother. "Not alone. I thought you knew. Lily was with her."

CHAPTER 18

I sat down. "I don't remember. You'd better tell me."

My father nodded. We looked at each other straight on for possibly the first time that weekend, neither of us looking away.

He said, "I was at the inquest. It—Kathy's death—was ugly. She ingested a glass of cleaning solvent. Ammonia of some kind. She was taking a bubble bath, and apparently had the glass all ready next to the tub. She drank half of it—more wasn't required. It burned out her throat, and she sank down under the water. The actual cause of death was drowning. There was water in her lungs.

"And Lily . . . Well, Kathy had locked the door to the attic but Lily knew where the key was. She had sneaked in before. She liked to hang out here when Kathy wasn't in."

Now, that sounded like Lily to me. "So she thought Kathy was out?" I asked.

"I think so," said my father. "Her testimony was a little confused. She was only seven. The judge was very gentle with her."

"What did she see?" I asked.

"At first she didn't realize Kathy was there. The bathroom door was closed. Then she heard a noise . . . probably the glass crashing to the floor." My mother made a sound, a soft involuntary mew, and my father paused for a moment, glancing at her, before continuing.

"Lily said she burst into the bathroom—yelling 'Boo!' or something. The bathroom door wasn't locked. You understand that it would all have happened very quickly. Kathy would have been beneath the water already. Lily said she thought Kathy was playing a game, holding her breath under the water. But she didn't come up."

"Lily got all wet," said my mother. "She tried to pull Kathy out . . ."

The ice cream I'd eaten earlier threatened to push its way back up my throat.

"Lily even tried to pick up the glass," my father said. "But of course it had shattered on the tile when Kathy dropped it, so Lily's hands got cut up. And her knees . . . She kept saying it was her fault. Children that age, they often think they're responsible for everything."

I had a vivid picture of Lily kneeling on the shards by the tub, pulling desperately at Kathy. "Okay," I said. "That's enough." But then I thought of something else.

110

"This was about Kathy's boyfriend?" I asked. "The one who dumped her?"

"Yes," said my mother.

"Well," said my father, the stickler for detail, "that's what the inquest concluded. The letter from him was on the kitchen counter."

I asked, "Did Kathy write a note or something?"

"No," he said, then added, "I wish she had. It would have been . . . not easier, perhaps, but more final." He shrugged. "People usually leave letters, but not always. This could have been a sudden impulse. Probably Kathy didn't really intend to die. Just to get sick. To scare her boyfriend, perhaps. And maybe Vic and Julia, too. They'd been fighting."

I found myself staring across the room into the bathroom. Its door was ajar, and I could see the edge of the tub inside.

"Why were Vic and Julia fighting with Kathy?" I asked.

"They'd been fighting since she dropped out of college," my mother said. "She'd been commuting to U. Mass, Boston. Do you remember?"

"Something, yeah," I said. What I suddenly did remember were my mother's comments about it. *Julia won't pull her claws out of Kathy. Mark my words: That girl will never get away.*

"So they were angry at Kathy for dropping out of school?" I asked.

"Yes. They'd been letting her live here rent free. But when she dropped out and got a job, Julia said she had to start paying." My mother's tone dripped disapproval.

111

"That doesn't sound unreasonable," I said, and heard my father's grunt of agreement.

"She wasn't earning very much money," retorted my mother. "And I think, with a little understanding and support, she would have gone back to school. But Julia's attitude made her dig in harder. Julia always makes you want to do the opposite of what she says."

That was true. I moved on. "So they fought about college and about rent money? And Julia and Vic were in agreement?"

"Well," my mother said. "My brother . . ."

I waited.

"At first, Vic didn't take the rent money from Kathy. She'd give him a check and he'd deposit it, but then he'd give her back the cash. Julia didn't know."

"Tell him, Eileen," said my father.

"I was going to!" my mother said. But then she sighed. "Oh, God. This is embarrassing. David, it was my idea. Vic asked me about charging Kathy rent . . . he wasn't sure . . . so I told him to give Kathy back the money. Secretly."

"It was a spectacular piece of meddling," observed my father calmly. "Your mother outdid herself."

"I was only thinking of Kathy!" my mother protested.

"You were thinking of needling Julia, and you know it."

"Oh, and you're so perfect yourself!" Then her voice changed. "I've said I was sorry. I've said it again and again . . . to Vic, to Julia. I couldn't be sorrier."

"Julia found out?" I asked, even though I already knew. It explained so much.

112

"Naturally," said my father.

"Shut up, Stuart," said my mother. "Yes, David, she found out. Kathy told her—yelled it at her—in the middle of a fight."

I could picture it. Perhaps they had had that fight right here, in this living room. Perhaps Julia had said, *Your father and I . . .* and Kathy had flung back, *Dad doesn't agree with you! He agrees with me! Do you know what he does? Do you know . . .*

It was odd. I could almost hear her. Almost see her as she screamed at Julia, her shoulders stiff like Lily's so often were. *Kathy?* I thought. *Kathy, are you there? Are you here?*

I heard it then, plainly. Clearly. The humming.

"David?" said my mother.

I looked up. "Yes?"

"Julia has never forgiven me," my mother said. "But I am most sincerely sorry. I've told her. I told her then, and after Kathy . . . and I've written . . ." Her voice trailed off.

"I understand," I said.

"I *thought* I meant well. But your father is right, too. Julia and I . . . I'd gotten into the habit of, well, I was always trying to score points . . . It went too far. *I* went too far. I know that."

I said, "It's okay," and I heard her sigh. I listened as my mother told the rest of the story.

After the incident over the rent, Kathy had begun paying for real. Julia collected the checks, and kept a sharp eye on the checking account to ensure that Vic gave Kathy no extra money. My mother believed that this, and not Kathy's death, was the true beginning of

113

Vic and Julia's estrangement. And then Kathy's new boyfriend had entered the scene.

"He wasn't a nice Catholic boy," said my mother. "Or even a nice Jewish boy. But I don't know a lot about it. My brother . . . wasn't talking very much to me right then. He had long hair. The boy, I mean." Her eyes skittered away from my own hair, longer than it had ever been. "An earring too. Of course no job. And of course they were . . ." She gave me a quick look, swallowed, and finished bravely. ". . . having sex."

It was an odd moment to realize I loved her, my sturdily Catholic—despite the conversion—mother. I grinned at her. For a second, as our eyes held, I thought we might both laugh. Then she ducked her head. "Well. It was all perfectly ordinary, really. Julia overreacted. Anyway, it only lasted three months. But by the end, nobody was talking, even to argue."

Nobody talking. Typical Shaughnessy. Typical Yaf—

I said quickly, "And then Kathy died."

"Yes," said my mother. "Yes."

That was all.

After a while, my parents went to bed, and I flung myself onto the sofa. Then I got up, and prowled into the bathroom; looked at the tub. It needed a good scrubbing. I had never bothered.

If I closed my eyes I could almost see Kathy there. See the shadow; hear the humming.

All at once I couldn't bear being in the house. I put on my running clothes and headed out, fast.

The Shaughnessy apartment was dark. The only indication that Vic and Julia were there was the fact that their bedroom door was closed.

Lily's door was also shut. For some reason I paused outside it for a few seconds. It wasn't all Lily's fault that she was so odd. Terrible things had happened in her short life.

I was halfway down the stairs when I realized that I hadn't asked my parents about Lily. What had been going on with her while Kathy quit school, got a job and a boyfriend, and fought with her parents? Very likely my mother and father would not have known. What was there to know about a seven-year-old? That she had been in second grade? That she had liked to sneak into the attic where her big sister lived, to play at being grown-up?

I should live here, Lily had said of the attic, on the day I moved in. *It's all wrong.*

And then I wondered: Why would she want to live in the place where she'd seen her sister die?

CHAPTER 19

On Monday, I found myself whistling as I arrived at medieval history. Raina had kissed me, gently, the night before when we got back from seeing the student films. For a long moment it confused me. I couldn't respond. And then I could.

It was so sweet.

I barely knew Raina. I didn't believe she could honestly be attracted to me. Most importantly, more deeply, it felt wrong to think I could be with her. Or anyone. Very wrong; evil, almost. There would always be Emily, and what had happened.

What I had done.

Still, irrationally, I felt amazingly good. I decided not to talk myself out of it yet.

I entered the classroom a full three minutes before the bell, and found Frank Delgado already slouched in his chair at the front. He was reading. Just as predictably, no one else, not even Dr. Walpole, had yet arrived.

"Hey," I said.

After a pause, Frank dog-eared a page and closed the book. After a longer pause, he nodded hello. Over his shoulder, I squinted down at the title of his book. *Zen and the Art of Motorcycle Maintenance.*

On impulse, I pulled out my Star Market card and offered it to him. He stared at it, and for a moment I thought he might not know about swapping. But then he grinned—nearly everyone did when you offered to swap—and pulled out his wallet. I gave him ELLIS O'DONNELL and he gave me JOANNE STANBRIDGE.

"That's new," I said, indicating the Zen book. "How are you doing with that other guy? Abu-something."

"Abulafia. Fine. What about you? Have you finished *The Guide for the Perplexed* yet?"

"I'm listening to it on tape," I said. "In the original Arabic." And then I laughed because, after all, Raina had kissed me.

Frank stared at me. I sat down next to him. I picked up the Zen book and looked through it a little. "You believe any of this?"

Frank said, "I *want* to believe."

It was a near-perfect imitation of David Duchovny as Fox Mulder. I almost choked. Frank looked at me blandly.

"You watch *The X-Files*?" I asked.

"Sometimes."

"I wouldn't have thought it would be your kind of thing," I said.

"Why not? Too weird?" His mouth twisted. "Not weird enough?"

I stifled another laugh. Frank noticed but didn't seem to mind. If I hadn't known better, I'd have thought there was the start of a smile on his face. "I don't know," I said. "It's TV. I guess I'm surprised you'd watch TV."

Frank stretched out his legs. "Why's that?"

"I'd have thought you'd think it's all crap," I said.

"A lot of it *is* crap," said Frank. "So I usually read something while I'm watching."

Now that was not a surprise. "I'm hooked on *The X-Files*," I found myself confessing.

Frank said, "I'm into *Looney Tunes*. I've seen every Road Runner cartoon multiple times."

I looked at him. He looked back. And then, as if on cue, we chorused together: "Wile E. Coyote. *Super-genius*."

"Brilliant stuff," said Frank.

"Yeah," I said.

But later that afternoon as I climbed the stairs to the Shaughnessy apartment, I was feeling itchy again, wary. Relief flooded through me when I didn't see or hear Lily. I had run into Lily the night before, when I came up after Raina kissed me.

Lily had been sitting on the floor of the living room, headphones jacked into the stereo, bare toes just visible beneath the hem of her flannel nightgown as she hugged her knees. Neither of us said a word, but I was conscious of the soft murmur of voices in the other end of the apartment. Vic and Julia, of course.

Lily's eyes tracked my progress across the room in

the near-dark. I felt them on the back of my neck as I fumbled with the doorknob of the attic stairs. I fancied that Lily could smell me from across the room. Could smell Raina's perfume. Incredibly, I'd felt a fiery blush rise on my neck and face. It seemed to take forever to get the door open and closed behind me. And even after I'd gotten myself upstairs, I'd imagined Lily listening from below, hearing my footsteps on my floor, which was her ceiling.

Why did Lily make me feel so uneasy? I had to get hold of myself. Had to be mature. I couldn't go on tiptoeing around, hoping not to see her. She lived here, and so did I. We were going to see each other. It was just a fact.

As I changed to go running, I thought again of my cousin Kathy. I pulled out the photo and looked at her. It was a senior-year photo; she had been my age, more or less. There was a certain defiance in her smile. I wondered about her boyfriend, the one with the long hair who'd dumped her. I wondered if she'd ever brought him home. I bet she had, especially after she'd begun paying rent. I bet she'd enjoyed bringing him home, leading him upstairs under the noses of Vic and Julia.

Had Vic and Julia been talking to each other then? Had Lily carried messages for them? What had the seven-year-old Lily thought of her big sister, the favorite child who had finally managed to lose her parents' favor?

And as I straightened up from tying my running shoes and leaned against the wall at an angle, balancing for calf stretches, an answer to my own question floated into my head. *She was glad. She was thrilled. Don't you see, she was suddenly the favorite.*

I couldn't help myself; I whipped around. And I saw—I swear I saw—the faint outline of the figure I'd seen and sensed many times before. A slender girl. Kathy. I knew now it was Kathy. I recognized her. I took in several deep, shallow breaths.

Then the figure was gone. I stared at the place it had been. I stared until my eyes felt raw. The late-afternoon sun sent weak rays through the windows and onto the floor. There was nothing there. There had never been anything there.

Ghosts were for entertainment. For television. For *The X-Files*. They were not part of real life. I, for one, emphatically did not believe. Ghosts could not be real. For if they were, I would surely not be haunted by my cousin Kathy. I would be haunted—as I deserved to be—by Emily.

I grabbed my keys and bolted down the stairs to run all the craziness out of myself.

CHAPTER 20

Over the few weeks that remained in the year, I saw Raina once or twice a week. It was casual; she did not kiss me again. Part of me was disappointed, but a larger part was relieved. I certainly made no move.

It was good, though, just hanging out with someone. We spent some hours together in her apartment, Raina drawing or painting, me working on college applications—due by January 15th. Even as I kept myself apart, I got to know *her* a little. She loved her myriad step- and half siblings, but was wary of her mother. She was fully capable of unplugging and forgetting her telephone for days on end. She ate canned soup every night with undiminished enjoyment. She'd had two significant boyfriends, one of whom she still had feelings for. "But, you know, he'll never leave El Paso," she said. "And I had to."

Raina didn't seem to need to discuss exactly what *our* relationship was, or where, if anywhere, it was going.

There was only one really bad incident. Once, I looked up and found that she was sketching me, in charcoal, when she was supposed to be working on a still life for school. I was furious—literally saw red—but she seemed sincerely surprised to discover what her hands had been doing. She stared at her drawing for some moments as if it astonished her, too.

And I—thank God, thank God—calmed down. Quickly. The red faded from before my eyes; the abyss receded. Nothing had happened. No reflexes had kicked in. I had not even moved. Nothing.

I knew then that Frank was right. Fear was never far from me.

"Come look," said Raina, oblivious.

After another moment, I did.

The still life she'd been working on was a winter piece: bare branch, pinecone, shallow bowl of water, a dried chrysanthemum. However, a broken face was intertwined with it. An eye blinked from the center of the pinecone. A nose lay alone on the table beside the branch. A mouth gasped for air at the bottom of the bowl of water.

My features. My face. One glance was enough. I looked away.

Raina moved her shoulders. "Well. You can have it." And she gave it to me. "I'm sorry. I told you I wouldn't do this."

Once I got upstairs, I tore it up and burned the fragments in the sink.

Outside, the days were short, the temperature dropped well below freezing and stayed there, and it snowed with extraordinary frequency and ferocity for Boston in December. Once or twice a week I shoveled the driveway and sidewalk with Vic, who insisted on joining me even though I said I could handle it.

"I'm not *that* old," he told me. "And with you helping, it's the right amount of exercise."

Vic was looking great. There was an air of cautious contentment about him. He held his shoulders straighter. And Julia, too, seemed different. She smiled at me on the few occasions I ran into her, and asked me about my day, and how my parents were.

"I can't believe you've always done the shoveling by yourself," I huffed at Vic. The latest snow had been wet and heavy. It stuck to my plastic shovel and was difficult to shift. "Haven't you ever thought of buying a snowblower?"

"Well, Lily often helps," Vic replied. He dumped his own shovelful of wet snow with an expert, economical arm movement. "You wouldn't think she could do much, but she's not bad."

"Oh," I said neutrally. Lily had not been conspicuous with a shovel after the last few storms. I heaved more snow onto the hillock we'd built at the far end of the driveway.

"Bend your knees more, you Southern boy," Vic advised me. He laughed when I misfired, tossing the snow into the street instead of on our mound. He said genially, "You're wondering where Lily is today? Well, I asked her to come out, but she said no." He looked a little sad, but then brightened. "It's to be expected. She's growing up. And she's been a little moody lately. Before you know it she'll be into those teenage years."

We continued shoveling in silence. I wondered if that truly was Vic's interpretation of Lily. *A little moody.* Were he and Julia blind? Didn't they understand that their reconciliation had upset Lily? Changed her life?

Involuntarily, I glanced up at the second floor of the house, where I could see the floral curtains framing the living room windows. I didn't really know if Lily was up there, watching Vic and me. But I thought so.

The very next night I came face-to-face with her.

I had spent the evening defending Fox Mulder on alt.tv.x-files, and then following a craving for potato chips over to Star Market. Coming home, I trudged upstairs in my boots as quietly as I could.

I saw Lily as I shucked my coat in the Shaughnessy hall. She was standing outside her parents' bedroom, with a drinking glass pressed between her ear and the wall.

I couldn't believe it. She was eavesdropping. No. She was *spying.*

She snapped around to face me. Slowly she lowered the glass, her fingers tight around it. For a second I thought she would hurl it at me. Instead, she gritted her teeth. She was in her threadbare flannel nightgown again.

"Lily?" I said softly. I held out my hand. "Give me the glass. I'll put it away."

For a long, long moment she didn't move. Then, still clutching the glass, she tilted her chin and walked slowly to the kitchen.

I followed uneasily. I watched her carefully rinse out the glass and place it in the dish drainer. There was only a night-light on by the sink; Lily was a gray shadow. I said her name again, quietly. "You shouldn't eavesdrop on your parents," I said. "It's wrong."

She didn't turn. Her voice even softer than mine, she said, "Who are *you* to tell me about right and wrong?"

Her words struck me in the throat like a knife.

"I don't care if you tell my parents," she added then, and the childish comment eased the pain her first had caused. Partly.

I forced myself to focus. Julia and Vic had a right to know about the kind of spying Lily was doing. But . . . well, this was all very tough on Lily, too, and her parents didn't appear to realize that. I said, "I won't tell them."

"I don't care if you do," Lily insisted. She straightened her shoulders, and turned, giving me a straight look before wrapping her arms around herself. She was shivering; it was too cold for her to be standing barefoot on the linoleum.

"Go to bed," I said. "You have school tomorrow."

Lily ignored me. "Do you know what they were doing?" she said. "Do you?"

Until that moment it actually hadn't occurred to me to wonder. I had assumed Lily was listening to a conversation, but . . . a picture formed in my mind.

"You do," Lily accused. She took a step toward me.

I groped frantically for something to say. "Look, Lily," I finally managed. "The best way to deal with, uh . . . parental sexuality is, uh, not to think about it."

Lily's face twisted with contempt. "You are just a jerk," she whispered. She took another step toward me, eyes narrowing. "Maybe your parents"—her voice slipped into perfect mimicry of mine—"experience parental sexuality. But mine *fuck.* That's what they're in there doing, right now. Okay?"

Something about hearing that word from Lily. And imagining Vic and Julia—

My shock must have been apparent. Lily laughed, scornfully. But then the scorn faded from her expression, and that other look returned. The betrayed look. The vicious look. And beneath all of that, the despair. The fear.

I wanted desperately to go upstairs to the attic, to crawl into bed and unconsciousness. I didn't understand Lily. I didn't trust Lily. She unnerved me. But—

Tomorrow, maybe, I'd talk to Vic. Find some gentle way of suggesting a therapist for Lily, who clearly needed to talk to someone.

"They never used to do it," Lily said, almost as if to herself. "But—they do it now. Why? *Why?*" She stared at me accusingly.

I had nothing to say. I turned to leave. I would deal with this, somehow, later.

But Lily darted across the kitchen and grabbed my arm. Her little nails pinched fiercely through my shirt. "It's all your fault," she said. "If you hadn't come here, this would never have happened. Things would still be the way they were." She brushed past me and disappeared down the hall. Her bedroom door clicked quietly shut.

After a minute I trudged on, upstairs to Kathy's attic, where I put on all the lights.

On the bedroom dresser was a little menorah that my mother had given me at Thanksgiving. Beside it was the unopened packet of candles. I suddenly realized it was the third night of Hanukkah.

I walked over to the dresser, opened the box of candles, and filled the menorah—not just with the candles for that night, but completely. Eight plus the *shammash*. Yellow, blue, red, fuchsia, green, orange, white, white, white. I lit them all. Then I sat on my bed—on Kathy's bed—for forty minutes in the blazing glare of the electric lights, and watched the flames flicker and dance and then, one by one, die.

Who was I to tell *anyone* about right and wrong?

CHAPTER 21

"Oh, leave Lily alone," Raina said. She reached past me for the turpentine, poured it liberally over the brushes massed in a small tin pail, and began scrubbing. The air stank.

I stared at her.

It had been a couple of days since I'd caught Lily spying on her parents. I still hadn't talked to Vic. The previous night, after trying to fall asleep, I'd gone out to Dolly's All-Night Restaurant over in Davis Square, eaten steak and eggs at the counter, swapped DIANA CURTIS for DEBBIE WILES, and returned to the house—feeling like I was sneaking in—around two A.M. The hallway through the Shaughnessy apartment was dark and silent. I'd gone upstairs, tried bed again, even fallen asleep for an hour. And over the course of the following day in school, I'd mentally rehearsed how I'd tell Raina the story of my encounter with Lily in the hall. Raina would be able to advise me about the best way to approach Vic and Julia. Women were good at stuff like that.

"But don't you think she needs help?" I said to Raina. "Don't you think her behavior is weird? That someone should do something?"

"Why you?" said Raina reasonably. "She has parents."

"But . . . they're—" I stopped.

Raina grabbed her cleaned brushes, dried them with a rag, and dumped them, bristles up, in an empty coffee can. "And, hey, didn't you tell her you *wouldn't* tell her parents? When I was a kid, I really hated being lied to." She began to dry her hands.

"Yeah, me too," I said automatically. But I thought, *Isn't getting help for Lily more important than that promise? Lily even said she didn't care if I told.* Of course I hadn't believed that.

"I'll think about it some more," I said. "I don't have to do anything right away."

Raina nodded. "Makes sense." She squinted toward the windows, gauging the light, the time left before sunset. It was a squint I knew. She wanted to do some work. I should not have felt dismissed, ignored—but I did.

I left.

It was almost dinnertime, but I didn't want to go upstairs. Everything else aside, all I had to eat there was a microwaveable frozen dinner. Early the next morning, I was due on a plane down to Baltimore for Christmas week vacation. I drove to Harvard Square and parked in an expensive garage. It was bitingly cold out. Above, the streetlights glared yellow; neon lights on stores

129

pulsed in counterpoint. I shoved my hands into my pockets, keeping my head down as I forced my way into the wind, worrying about Lily, wondering where to get food.

Just outside Tower Records, someone stepped right in front of me. "Hey."

I looked up. It was Frank Delgado, wearing shorts in the snow, and holding a Harvard Coop bag.

"Christmas shopping?" I asked, just to say something. I gestured at his bag.

"Yeah. You? Hanukkah, I mean?"

I had a fleeting thought of Vic and Julia and Lily, for whom I'd bought the most innocuous of gifts, and shook my head. "No. Just on my way to get some dinner."

Frank nodded, and I had an idea. I fished in my wallet and came out with the gold Visa card with my father's account number on it. I waved it in front of Frank. "Hey," I said. "Wanna come to dinner? Let's go somewhere good. It's on my father."

Frank regarded me carefully. "Are you drunk?"

"Can't you tell?" I said. "I'm drunk on life."

"I see," said Frank. He reached out for the Visa card and I let him have it. He read my name on the front; my signature on the back. Then he handed it back. "Let's go," he said, and fell into step beside me. We headed up JFK Street. "Have you heard of Upstairs at the Pudding?" Frank said. "It's over on Holyoke."

"Is it good?" I asked.

"Never been."

"Is it expensive?"

"Yeah."

"Sounds perfect," I said.

The maitre d' didn't blink at Frank's shorts or at his head. We were shown very politely to an excellent corner table. The waiter said cheerfully, "A soft drink to start?"

That killed the idea Frank's comment had raised. Oh, well. I asked for root beer, and Frank for water. The waiter brought a basket of bread and a cruet of olive oil. I ordered appetizers for us both, and the large filet mignon for my entree. Frank ordered the grilled vegetable plate. Then I said to Frank, who was busy wiping up olive oil with a piece of focaccia: "Why'd you shave your head?"

He put the bread in his mouth, chewed thoughtfully, and swallowed. He drank some water. Then he said, "Because it upset people."

A reasonable answer. "And why do you keep it shaved?"

"To upset people."

"You enjoy that?" I asked.

"Don't you?" Frank countered.

"No," I said, and I realized I was telling the exact truth.

"Too bad," Frank said softly, and I stared at him because of course he was right. It would be easier.

Frank ate more bread. So did I. He said, "I like watching what happens when people get upset. That's when you find out who they really are."

We finished off the bread in the basket, and the lemon artichoke heart appetizer, and the cheese things, and called for more bread and more spring water for Frank.

I asked Frank where he was applying to college, and he asked me. I asked him if money was a factor, and he said yeah, his mother was a teacher. He asked me the same question and, feeling guilty, I said no. We exchanged S.A.T. scores. His were better than mine.

"Do you really want to go to college?" I asked.

"Yes," he said. "High school . . . well. Let's just say I'm ready to move on."

I said, "I'd rather get a job."

"Doing what?"

"I don't know. It doesn't matter."

"It should," said Frank.

I shrugged. Maybe if there were something I wanted to do, it would matter.

Our dinners arrived. I ate my steak. Frank vacuumed up his vegetables. Halfway through the meal, he looked up at me and said, "I believe it gets better. I really do."

"You *want* to believe," I said, and he grinned. But I thought, *You're not me.*

We ate four desserts between us, and the bill was satisfyingly high. I signed for it and, while I was in my wallet, swapped Frank JANE KURTZ for BOB SULLAWAY. I dropped Frank off at a double-decker house just over the Cambridge-Somerville line, and drove resignedly back to the Shaughnessy house.

It was just before nine o'clock, and Julia was alone in the kitchen. Her surprise was obvious when I came in and greeted her. But she said hello cordially enough, turning aside from the potato she was dicing, and wiping her hands on her apron. "It's just a stew for tomorrow," she said when I apologized for interrupting her. "I've made it a thousand times."

132

"Smells great," I said.

The tiniest smile appeared on Julia's face. "Well, Vic likes it. I always serve it on the second day. I don't know why, but it tastes better after it's been reheated." And she touched her hand briefly, unconsciously, to her gray, stiffly coiffed hair.

I knew that gesture. It was commonplace at school, among the flirty flocks of teenage girls. I'd seen Emily use it a thousand times. I could not quite believe I'd just seen it from Julia.

Lily was right about her parents.

"So, you're off tomorrow for Baltimore," Julia was saying. "Give my best to Eileen and Stuart. Vic will pick you up at the airport next Sunday afternoon. He knows when your flight gets in? Good." She picked up her knife and began on a new potato, slanting me another one of those incongruous teenage girl looks. "So," she said, "I hear you're dating the girl downstairs?"

"Well," I answered, "I wouldn't say—"

But Julia continued chattily. "Vic . . ." Her voice lingered. "Vic says Eileen and Stuart met her when they were here at Thanksgiving; he says they liked her. She's a good tenant. Quiet, always pays the rent on time."

She paused a second, and then added, surprisingly, "Why don't you bring her up to dinner sometime, so we can get better acquainted? I'll make a roast. I saw in the circular that they're on sale all next week. Raina eats meat, doesn't she? Or is she one of those vegetarians?"

This was not a Julia I knew. This was someone else.

"I think Raina eats meat," I said slowly. "But I don't know if—"

"Good. Then after you come back, we can pick a night. It'll be fun."

Fun. Right. "Okay," I said, not seeing a way out. Maybe Raina wouldn't want to come.

"Vic will be so pleased," said Julia. She nodded, and I said good-bye and retreated.

So much for telling Julia about Lily. I couldn't do it. I just couldn't, not then. I wasn't prepared to break into Julia's love affair with her husband by telling her that her daughter had been spying on them.

I would tell Vic. After New Year's. When I got back.

CHAPTER 22

My last night in Baltimore, New Year's Day night, I had a dream. I was standing with Frank Delgado in an early Gothic church. I recognized it: Rothenburg, a nearly perfectly preserved medieval town in Bavaria. Dr. Walpole had shown us slides of it. And although she was not there, I could hear her voice saying: "The altar is circa 1490. It is dedicated to St. Francis."

Frank snorted and I turned to face him. He was dressed like a monk, his bald head for once looking appropriate. From his rope belt hung a rosary. Carefully, in both hands, he held up a thick, dusty library book. I recognized the letters but could not decipher them. Frank winked. "It's *The Guide for the Perplexed*," he said. Then he held out a Star Market card. "Swap?"

I reached into my pocket, scrabbling frantically, but I couldn't find a card. And then Frank disappeared, and Raina, wearing tight jeans and a T-shirt, stood in his place. She took my hand and pulled. "Let's climb to the top of the tower," she said. "There's a view."

"No, come to the torture museum," said Lily, who was suddenly beside me, clutching my other hand with remarkable strength. Raina disappeared. And Lily and I were inside the cold wet stone walls of a dungeon. "Over there," said Lily, pointing to an iron maiden lying open on its back behind a velvet rope. "Come see." She let go of my hand and ran forward, swinging on the rope, peering inside the iron maiden, swinging back, forward, back again.

I walked up beside her. I looked inside the iron maiden and saw the tiny bathtub from the attic in Cambridge, filled with clear water. Kathy lay immersed in it, her arms crossed on her breast, flowers strewn about her. She was impaled on spikes, bloodless, and quite dead.

Lily giggled. "It's me," she said. "I—"

"Shut up," I said. I grabbed her up in my arms, ignoring her squirming, and strode through the stone corridors of the museum, shoving through crowds of tourists, calling for Raina, for Frank. And then for Vic and Julia. And then for my parents. And then—my throat raw—for Emily.

Emily. Emily, Emilyemilyemily . . .

No one was there but strangers. And then even they disappeared, and I was alone with Lily—now screaming, kicking, and biting—in my arms.

I forced myself awake. I was sweating; had thrown off the heavy quilt. I reached out automatically for the bedside lamp, but I was in Baltimore and the nightstand was on the other side of the bed. Finally I found the lamp and, sitting up, switched it on. The sudden light hurt my eyes, so that for a moment I didn't see her. Then I did.

No shadow. No humming. No.

Down by my feet, sitting on the edge of the bed, was my cousin Kathy. As in my dream, she was pale. Her hair was wet. Her eyes, narrowed and anxious and more than a bit fierce, met mine. She put out a paper-white hand, and her lips moved. "Lily," she whispered rustily. "Help Lily."

One moment she was solid. The next—she dissolved. I squeezed my eyes shut tightly and opened them again, and there was nothing there.

I had imagined it. Surely I had imagined it.

I stumbled into the bathroom, and immersed my head in cold water in the sink. Then I got dressed for running, and went out into the predawn cold on a long route that—like every other outing that week in Baltimore—went nowhere near Emily and Greg's house.

It had been a strange, unreal week, full of places not visited, people not seen, conversations not held. All my old friends were probably home from their colleges, but of course I hadn't called them. I couldn't.

Everywhere I looked, I saw Emily.

I stayed in, watching TV, reading. Toward the end of the week I finally sat down and finished my college applications—to five big faceless medium-ranked city schools that the year before would have been, at best, safety selections—and e-mailed them in. That last morning, after the nightmare, I printed out the final list of places I'd applied to and handed it to my parents over breakfast.

"What about Yale? Stanford? And—" began my mother, but then she stopped, biting her lip.

"It's a done deal," I said. She didn't sigh, but I heard it anyway.

"What are you thinking about for a major these days?" asked my father.

"Psychology," I said, surprising myself. I had written "undecided" on all my applications. For a few minutes there was only the overly loud sound of my teeth crunching on Cheerios.

"You could do with a little less self-pity," said my father.

I was watching the last few Cheerios drift around in the bowl of milk. It took everything I had right then to turn my head and look straight at my father. He looked just as he always did at the breakfast table: *Washington Post* carefully sectioned beside him, coffee cup in hand, the thick glasses masking his real thoughts. Even dressed in casual Sunday clothes, he looked formal.

"Your point is?"

"You need to get on with your life," said my mother urgently. "Let the past go. Stop . . . stop . . . ," she faltered.

"Stop feeling responsible for what I did?"

"I . . . I just don't see why you have to let it change your whole life . . ." She stopped again.

"I'm not," I said reasonably. "I'm finishing high school. Going to college. What more do you want?"

"Yes," she said. "But I'm just afraid you . . . you're not—"

"Not what?" I said.

"I don't know," said my mother. "I don't know." She put her hands over her eyes.

"Do *you* know?" said my father to me. "Do you know what you're doing to yourself? Do you know why?"

I didn't reply. I thought at him: *Why can't you understand that everything's changed forever?*

He didn't hear me. We sat in silence.

Eventually I pushed my chair back from the table and left the room. A couple of hours later they drove me to the airport, and a couple of hours after that, I was once more in Boston, where, at least, Emily was less . . . less present.

Sitting in the car with Vic, I found myself glad to be back. There were some people I liked here. Raina. And, incredibly, Frank Delgado.

Before I'd left for Baltimore, I had promised myself I'd tell Vic about Lily's behavior. And now I'd had orders from Kathy's ghost—or, if you preferred, from a hallucination conjured up by my paranoid and guilt-ridden subconscious—to do so. *Help Lily.* It couldn't have been clearer, really.

But looking at Vic, hearing his chatter about how he and Julia had gone ballroom dancing on New Year's Eve, my courage failed. I'd wait for a few days, I decided. I'd see how Lily was acting. Maybe she was adjusting.

I would give her a little more time before I told Vic.

CHAPTER 23

"**W**ow," said Raina, as she, and I, and Vic, and Julia clustered somewhat uneasily in Julia's kitchen the following Friday evening. "That roast smells amazing."

Julia smiled, visibly pleased. She had meant it about inviting Raina and me to dinner. She'd delivered a formal note to Raina right after I got back from Baltimore, and a few days later, there we were. I'd wondered if I needed to warn Raina that Julia thought we were dating, but in the end, I couldn't figure out how to do it without possibly triggering a conversation I didn't want to have.

But Raina seemed straightforwardly delighted merely at the prospect of a large meal. I could hardly believe this was the same person who ate can after can of tomato soup. She prowled the kitchen like a panther, sniffing ecstatically. "Fresh bread! Yum!"

140

"It's just the basic white loaf recipe from *Joy of Cooking*," replied Julia. She wore an apron. Her hair was carefully styled.

"Wine, dear?" said Vic.

"Oh, yes." Julia held out her glass and Vic, courtly and freshly shaven, poured her half a glass of merlot. Julia grinned at him and he grinned back. Raina smiled at me, an aren't-they-cute smile. I did my best to return it. Vic poured us some wine, too.

"Not too much," said Julia coyly. "They're underage."

"A little wine at home never hurt anyone," said Vic. "To the new year," he toasted, and we clinked glasses.

Down the hall, Lily's bedroom door was closed. I hadn't asked if she was joining us, but I'd assumed she would be.

As if she'd read my mind, Julia said, "I fed Lily earlier. She's too young for—you know—a *formal* dinner party. She wouldn't enjoy it."

"Oh," I said. I had seen Lily several times that week, and she had been impeccably polite to me each time. It made me glad of my decision not to say anything to Vic about her. Even so, I was relieved she would not be at dinner that night watching me and Raina.

We moved into the dining room, where the table was set for four. I sat down where Julia indicated, at the foot of the table, with Raina on my left. Julia sat next to Vic. I remembered sitting here at this table when I had first arrived. Then, Vic and Julia had sat apart. Lily had been across the table from me then, sitting between her parents.

"Maybe Lily can join us for dessert?" I said impulsively.

"We'll see," said Julia. "Vic, could you carve the roast? Who likes rare meat?"

"I do," said Raina.

After a while, I succeeded in forgetting Lily. The meal was good, and Vic was in a voluble mood. He related the history of rent control in Cambridge to Raina. "They forced us to bring it to a statewide vote," he said, stabbing his fork in the air. "There was no understanding of a property owner's rights! How did they expect me to pay my taxes and keep the place up?"

"Don't get excited, dear," said Julia. "It's over now."

"Thank God," said Vic. He turned again to Raina. "Even the president of the city council was in a rent-controlled apartment. It was obscene."

"Terrible," said Raina. She accepted more mashed potatoes.

Vic frowned and leaned forward. "Not that I'd ever vote Republican, you understand," he said. "Not in a national election. I couldn't go that far."

"Certainly not," said Raina. "David, could you just pass the butter? Thanks."

We had a nice time. I was astonished. There was real warmth in the room. Julia's candles guttered low on the table. I ate two helpings of roast beef and lost track of how many Raina had. Raina explained supermarket card swapping to a doubtful Julia; Vic confessed shyly that he'd been swapping for months. Under direct questioning, Raina talked cheerfully about her complicated family: parents; one stepmother; two stepfathers, and a grand total of twenty-three siblings, counting wholes and steps and halfs and by-previous-or-later-marriages.

I saw Vic glance at Julia. "That must be hard on you," he said to Raina. "It's best if people don't split up, I think. Marriage is forever."

"Well, I was too young to remember my parents together," said Raina. "And I understand. People change, after all. Stuff happens. You've got to go on."

There was a little silence. Then Julia said, quietly and with dignity, "Things happened to us, too. But you can survive together, if you try."

"And go on," said Vic. "Together." He stretched his hand openly over the table toward Julia. She clasped it. There were little circles of pink on her cheeks. "Well," she said. She released Vic's hand and, with a little bustle, got up from the table. "Who wants coffee or tea? David?" Her eyes brushed over my face quickly.

"Thank you, Julia," I said. "Coffee." Julia left, with Vic.

I felt Raina touch me quickly on the arm. "They're so sweet together," she whispered. "Oh, I like them."

I did too, right then. Even Julia. Even though I was also uncomfortable. Even though I was thinking of Lily. I smiled at Raina. "There's another slice of bread. Want it?"

"Well, if you insist," said Raina.

After dessert—Julia refused help with the cleanup—Raina said to me, offhandedly, "Walk me downstairs?"

"Okay," I agreed. We said good night. "I'll be right back," I told Julia, but the back of my neck burned a little bit as I opened the door to the front stairs and ushered Raina before me.

Raina didn't say anything as we went downstairs. Neither did I. I was suddenly very conscious of her.

She fumbled a little with her keys, and, laughing, handed them to me. But the door pushed open before I even had the key turned.

"I must have forgotten to pull it completely closed," said Raina. Her cheeks were flushed from the cold air, and maybe, too, from the wine. I was feeling light-headed myself.

I looked right into her lovely eyes. "Well, good night," I said, but my feet didn't move.

Raina said, "Why don't you come in for a minute?"

My feet did work, after all.

Her living room was eerie in the dark. The small of my back itched. I adjusted to the lack of light; the portraits were shadows on the walls. I whispered, "I feel like your pictures are watching us."

Raina laughed softly. "Maybe they are." She was almost exactly my height. And close, close.

An eternity passed. I could hear our breathing synchronize. Then Raina reached over, delicately, and traced my cheekbone with one finger. I didn't move. "I'm curious, David," she murmured. "Are you?"

I felt my head nod. I stepped closer.

I kissed her. It was gentle, investigative. The kind of kiss Emily and I had exchanged, a lifetime ago, when everything was new and I never dreamed anything could go wrong.

Then I kissed Raina again. And she kissed me. And I forgot Emily. Forgot myself. For what felt like years, I forgot absolutely everything except how wonderful—how good—how miraculous—

A light switch snapped. The living room exploded with the glaring light of the three bulbs in the naked fixture overhead.

I knew before I moved, before I looked. I felt Raina's body, suddenly stiff against me, her face in my hands, her arms around me. I knew, but I didn't want to look. I knew.

Lily.

I opened my eyes. I let go of Raina. I looked across the brightly lit room at Lily, who was standing in the frame of the bedroom door, her hand still positioned on the light switch. Her other hand held a key ring that I recognized. Vic kept it on a hook upstairs in the pantry.

Raina had not forgotten to lock her apartment door.

"I just wanted to say hello," said Lily. "Since I didn't get a chance at dinner." She paused, looking at us. Then she smiled. I remembered her with the glass outside her parents' bedroom. And what she'd said, then. It made me feel filthy.

As if she knew, Lily laughed. Then she ran lightly out, leaving the front door open.

Raina exhaled.

"That was Lily," I said needlessly. "She must have come in while we were having dinner." And then, when Raina didn't reply, the words broke out of me: "You told me not to talk to her parents."

Raina had wrapped her arms around herself. "I guess I was wrong," she said. She smiled a little, crookedly. "Well," she began. "Kids—"

I stepped farther away. "I'd better leave," I said. "Maybe it's just as well. I don't know what I was thinking."

She looked at me. The portraits looked at me.

"Good night," I said, and bolted.

Somehow I made it up the flight of stairs to the Shaughnessy apartment. Somehow I walked through their living room, past Vic and Julia, who were watching television from the sofa. Past Lily, who was sitting on the floor at their feet.

"Good night, David," called Lily sweetly.

"Sleep tight," added Julia. Out of the corner of my eye I saw Vic wave.

I couldn't reply. Somehow I got the door to the attic open, and in I went. Finally I got to the attic. Kathy's attic. I turned on every light in the place.

CHAPTER 24

That night, I did some work for school. Then I went online, read a ton of new stuff on alt.tv.x-files, and posted. *What you louts aren't getting*, I wrote, *is that Mulder wants his arid life. Can't you accept that maybe he's right about his responsibility for what happened to Samantha?* I knew they wouldn't listen, however. They never did. I accepted it.

By four A.M. I found myself prowling the apartment, looking in corners for Kathy. I knew that she had to be around someplace. If she wanted me to help Lily, then she could tell me what to say to her parents. But I didn't see her, or even hear the humming.

I did my level best not to think about Raina, and the expression on her face, under the glaring light, when I said good night. I didn't blame her. Nonetheless, I was doing the right thing. For a moment, I had forgotten myself, but she couldn't be anything other than a casual friend.

I would force myself to say something to Vic and Julia in the morning.

My eyes felt like peeled eggs when, finally, morning came. I heard Vic and Julia in the kitchen, and my feet took me downstairs. My mouth opened, and it said that there was something I wanted to talk to them about. In private. Upstairs.

I sat them on my sofa but I didn't sit down myself. Then I did, in the chair opposite them. Then I got up again.

"David, what's the matter?" asked Vic. "You said it was about Lily?"

"Yes." I exhaled, and then said, "Last night . . . after dinner . . . when I went downstairs with Raina . . . well. Lily was there. In Raina's apartment, hiding. And after a few minutes, uh, she jumped out and surprised Raina and me."

"Oh," said Vic. He looked at Julia. He shrugged a little.

"Victor," said Julia sternly. "Don't you see? She shouldn't have gone in there! Raina pays rent. We'll have to talk to Lily." She turned to me. "And you must tell Raina to lock her door, you know."

"The door was locked," I said. "Lily took the key from the pantry and let herself in before us."

Julia frowned. "Are you sure?"

"Yes."

"We'll have to move the keys somewhere else," said Julia decisively. She raised her hands and shoulders in a shrug, met my eyes. "Lily was probably feeling left out, you know, because of dinner. But I will definitely

148

speak to her about this. It's extremely rude behavior and I will tell her so. Vic?"

"Oh, yes," said Vic. "It's good of you to tell us, David." He got up, put out a hand to help Julia.

"Wait," I said, and they paused. "She . . . she was eavesdropping on me and Raina. She hid in the bedroom until we came in."

"Yes, I understand that," said Julia, flushing a bit.

"I mean—" I fumbled, but Julia cut me off.

"I understand, David." Her tone made it clear that I was not to continue. She averted her face, but in profile I could still see the slight twitch in her jaw. I looked at Vic.

"She's a kid, David," he said. "Curious . . . you know. We'll talk to her." His eyes slid away from mine. "Don't worry about it."

"We do apologize for her," said Julia formally. She smoothed her skirt, and got up.

"But . . . ," I said. *She's been spying on you, too.* The words formed in my mind but I found I couldn't say them. "But . . ."

"Yes, David?" said Julia. She looked at me full face now, and suddenly it was the old Julia there in her eyes, the Julia who had for years waged a cold war in her own house, the Julia who had not wanted me there.

This time I stared right back. "I think Lily should see a child psychiatrist," I said. "I know you don't want to hear it, but there have been other incidents, too. You must know it yourselves . . . she's not a happy child. She needs some kind of help."

Julia raised her chin. After a pause, she spoke quietly, evenly. "How dare you?"

"Look, Julia," I said. "I'm telling you frankly what I think because I want to help. We're family, after all, and I—"

"Family!" said Julia. "Family! *You!*"

I glanced at Vic for help, but he had shoved his hands in his pockets and was looking down.

"Come on," I said to Julia. "Lily is my cousin. I'm truly concerned—" Julia shook her head in patent disbelief, and I stopped. I watched her take a deep breath.

She pointed her chin at me. "I stopped putting up with your mother's interference years ago, and I'm not going to put up with yours, either. Not for a minute. Not in my house."

I glanced at Vic.

"And don't you go looking at Vic! He knows just as I do what interfering behavior like yours and your mother's can do to us if we let it." She grabbed my gaze with hers and held it. "We're not going to let it, David. Not this time. Do you understand me? You are not going to interfere with my family. Those are the terms under which I am allowing you to live here. In my house."

I knew then, seeing how Julia's cheeks flamed, how useless anything I might say to her would be. I knew it quite clearly.

"Vic, listen to me," I said. "Julia misunderstood me. I know there have been problems between my parents and you in the past, but this has nothing to do with that. I am simply worried about Lily, and—"

Vic wouldn't look at me. "Eileen was worried about

Kathy," he said softly. "But Julia is right. It would have been better if she hadn't been. It might—who knows?—it might have made all the difference."

I winced for my mother. "This is not the same," I persisted.

Vic shrugged. "Maybe. Maybe not." He looked at his wife, not at me. "I have to agree with Julia on this, David. Why don't you just leave Lily alone? That would be best, I think. I'm sure."

"We will hide the key ring," said Julia crisply. "I do take your point on that, David." But the way she glared at me told me that she was sure it was my fault.

I didn't know. I went out for a run on the sanded and salted streets, past all the piles of dirty snow, in the gray day. I ran for two hours or more. I ran until my lungs ached with the cold and I really couldn't anymore.

Maybe I was making it up; maybe Lily didn't need help. At the thought, I heard the humming again—urgent, buzzing.

Then it broke off.

CHAPTER 25

The instant I arrived back at the house, Raina's door shot open and she stuck her head out. "Get in here," she said. It was not an invitation; it was a command. When I hesitated, she added, "Now!"

She stood in front of me with her fists on her hips. "What exactly did you say to your aunt about last night?" she demanded. "Because she was just here, and she as much as called me a slut!"

I stared. "I . . . nothing much. I told her that Lily came in here. Stole the keys, hid here. Spied on us." But I had paused a little, and Raina picked right up on it.

"There's something you're not telling me. What is it?"

"She . . . my aunt may have *thought* we were—"

"What? Rolling around on the floor? Well, that's ironic."

I flushed. "I'm sorry—"

"She said horrible things to me. I'm a terrible example to her daughter. 'Bohemian.' Behind Raina's barely controlled voice, I could almost hear Julia's.

I flexed my shoulders. "Look, Julia has her own ideas. You shouldn't take it personally—"

She cut me off. "Oh, please. Listen, ordinarily I wouldn't care what anyone thought, but in this case . . ." She grabbed a piece of closely printed paper out of her back pocket and thrust it at me. "Do you know what this is?"

I examined it. "Your lease . . ."

"It's a tenant-at-will lease. You know what that means? It means I can leave anytime, so long as I give one month's notice. You know what else it means? That your aunt can kick me out anytime, with the same one month's notice!" Raina was panting now, and I thought I saw tears at the corners of her eyes. "Do you know how hard it was to find a place that was big enough, and cheap enough, and that got enough light? Do you know how hard it would be to find another place in the middle of winter? Do you know how expensive this town is? I'm not made of money!"

"But they wouldn't—"

"Your aunt made it very clear they would!"

"I can't believe—" I stopped. I did believe.

Raina wasn't finished. "And you! I don't get you. I just don't understand, and I'm tired of trying. It's not worth it. There are guys in this world who aren't messed up." She paused. Unexpectedly, a smile nudged at the corner of her mouth. "Okay, well. I don't know any. Yet." She sighed. The smile faded.

153

I didn't respond.

Raina said, quietly, "David Yaffe, what's with you? Honestly."

I owed her an explanation. I did. I said, with difficulty, not looking at her, "I love . . . loved Emily."

It was the truth, if not the entire truth. I couldn't tell her how frightened I was all the time. Not of Raina. Of myself.

Powerful, Lily had called it. But I didn't dare to give it a name.

There was a little pause. "Okay," said Raina. "You'd better leave. I'll . . . we'll . . . I'll see you around, okay? I like this place. I don't want to upset your aunt. You understand."

"Yeah," I said. I did understand, and I even thought it was best. Still . . .

I said, "See you around."

I felt empty, and yet at the same time there was something pushing at my chest. Something big. I had to get it out. I burst in on Julia and Vic and—because of course my wonderful luck was holding—Lily. The happy family was playing a cozy game of War at the kitchen table.

"Raina says you threatened to evict her," I said to Julia.

All three heads swiveled at once to face me. Vic looked a little embarrassed. He put a hand down over his pile of cards. His fingers tapped uneasily. "David. Don't overreact. It's just, uh, just—"

"This is our house," said Julia. "Our rules. You will abide by them while you live under our roof." She turned away. "One, two, three, go." They all three slapped down a card. Lily took the trick.

I stayed right where I was. "This morning we agreed—"

"We agreed," said Julia, "that you were just like your mother."

"Um," said Vic. He pushed back his chair from the table. "Julia, Lily. If you'll just excuse me for a moment. David . . ." He gestured toward the living room. "Maybe if you and I could talk alone?"

"Remember what we discussed, Victor," said Julia sharply.

"Of course," said Vic. He put a hand on Lily's shoulder. "I'll be right back, and then we'll get on with the game."

"Okay," said Lily. She smiled sweetly up at him. "Mommy and I will just wait for you," she said. She slanted the merest glance at me. Then, as she bent over her pile of cards, she said, "This is the most fun I've had in ages."

Like an automaton, I followed Vic into the living room, and then, at his signal, upstairs. He didn't look me in the face. "We talked to Lily," he said. "I know she shouldn't have been there at all . . . but she's only eleven and kids get into stuff . . . and when she told us what you were doing, you and that girl . . . well." He had to clear his throat. "Well. Uh. This is our house, like Julia says, and . . . well, this is our house."

I said, "But Raina and I were just kissing—"

"Lily told us what you were doing!" Vic was

suddenly beet red with—anger? Embarrassment? Both?

This was awful, but I had to know. "Vic, what *exactly* did Lily—"

"Enough!" Vic roared. The sound of his own voice seemed to surprise him. He repeated, doggedly, "This is our house. We have a right to . . . to protect our daughter from any . . . any bad influences."

Bad influences. That sounded like Julia. "Why don't you evict *me*, then?" I said bitterly, and knew immediately from Vic's silence that he and Julia had discussed it. Panic filled me. I was surprised by its depth. I couldn't leave. Where would I go? My parents didn't want me. They had sent me away.

"Vic," I said finally. "I have to tell you. Lily was spying on you and Julia, like she spied on me and Raina." At last I had said it. "I came in one evening and caught her outside your bedroom. She was listening to you and Julia with a glass. You were, uh . . . She said you were . . ." I stopped.

Vic's mouth moved like a fish's.

I continued. "She's been really unhappy since Thanksgiving," I said. "Since you and Julia got back together. That night when she was listening to you both, after I caught her she said some stuff to me . . ." As Vic listened, everything poured out of me in a great stream. I told Vic exactly what Lily had said about her parents that night in the hallway. I backtracked and told him about the time I'd come across Lily sitting on the stairs, all alone, while Vic and Julia laughed together inside. I said, "It stands to reason she would be sort of screwed up. After seeing Kathy die like that.

156

And then, you know, you and Julia not talking, and Lily carrying messages. Lily's in trouble. You can see that. Anybody can see that."

Vic listened so well that I only just barely caught myself before I told him about the humming shadow. About Kathy. About her telling me, *Help Lily*.

And when I finished, Vic said, carefully, "But Lily seems fine to me. She asked Julia and me to play cards with her today. We were having a good time."

"She's faking," I said positively. I felt hugely relieved, now that I'd told. "Deep inside, she's very angry. Confused. She needs to talk to a good therapist."

"Uh-huh," said Vic. He took a step back, away from me. "I'll think about this, David. I'll think about what you've said."

"That's all I ask," I said. "Thanks. Thanks for listening."

"Okay," said Vic. "Um. Okay."

He gave me one last look before he left.

CHAPTER 26

The next two weeks were quiet. Too quiet. My initial relief that Vic had at least listened to me faded. In my mind, I replayed the tape of my rant to him, and I was filled with vague doubts. But I had told Vic the truth. He had listened. He had.

Why was it so quiet?

I focused on school. Not wanting to see the Shaughnessys, not wanting to run into Raina even by accident, I started going over to the Cambridge Public Library after school, to study—or sometimes just to look at magazines and things—in the main reading room. Frank Delgado was often there too. We didn't talk much, but I began to look for him whenever I arrived. I took to giving him a ride home. Two or three times we got slices together at a little Greek pizza place across the street from the library.

Then, on a Thursday night, I got back to a dark house at eight o'clock. Upstairs in Kathy's apartment, I turned on my computer. Which refused to boot up. It took me a few minutes to figure out that the hard drive had been wiped.

Everything—operating system, programs, data files—was gone.

I took one comprehensive look around the apartment and pounded back downstairs, yelling Lily's name. But no one replied; the second floor was utterly deserted.

Okay, I thought. *Okay.* I took a deep breath. This was just like before, with Raina; but this time Lily had taken the key to the attic apartment. She had let herself in sometime that day. She had trashed my computer. There was nothing to be done about that. But I could stop her from doing anything else. I could get that spare key from the pantry where all the keys were stored. Then I would talk to Vic again. I would show him the computer.

I went down the hall and into the kitchen pantry. For some reason Vic had not updated the electricity in there; I needed to pull a string hanging from a low-wattage bulb set into the ceiling.

The pantry was filled with shelves from floor to ceiling, each of which was carefully lined with pages of *The Boston Globe* and fully stocked with canned goods. I counted nearly two dozen cans of lentil soup and a dozen of corn, and that was just to start. On a whim, I checked the top of a can with a finger. No dust. One amazing housekeeper, Julia.

On the left, at shoulder height, a series of hooks had been screwed into the wall; key rings hung there, each meticulously labeled. Cellar, front and back outside doors, Raina's first-floor apartment, the second-floor apartment, Vic's car, file cabinet, even tiny keys for luggage. And yes, there was a spare key for my apartment. I grabbed it, and held it in my fist.

There was no sound. I don't know why I suddenly knew Lily was in the kitchen behind me. I turned slowly and looked at her. I kept my face impassive. Down the hall I could see the open door to her bedroom; it had been closed when I'd come past before. Had she been in there in the dark? I was a fool, there was no doubt about it.

"My parents went out to a movie," Lily said politely. "Can I help you?"

I did not yell. "Why?" I said to her.

The tiniest smile curled the corner of her mouth. "Why what?"

"You trashed my computer."

Lily smiled fully. "You're crazy."

"Why did you trash my computer?"

"You're *craaazy*," sang Lily. "My parents think you're *craaazy*." She hugged herself.

Involuntarily, my eyes flicked to the row of drinking glasses standing on a shelf. "Spying again, Lily?" I said.

"You're going to have to leave," said Lily. "They think you're nuts. Making stuff up. Imagining things about me. Plus, I'm scared of you. I told them so."

I looked into her fearless face. Slowly, finally, her words penetrated fully. *Crazy. You're crazy.*

I swallowed. The slight unease I'd felt since telling Vic what I thought about Lily filled me again. In my mind's eye I saw Vic take a step back away from me. I heard him say, *Uh-huh.*

160

"You trashed my computer," I said stubbornly. "Why?"

"Why would I do a thing like that?" Lily leaned a little closer to me, and her voice dropped to a whisper, "I'm just a kid. I wouldn't even know how."

"You trashed—"

"What are you going to do?" Lily asked. "Dust for fingerprints?" She rocked, slightly, from side to side.

I clenched my hand on the key. "Get out of my way," I said. "And keep out of—" I could not say, *my place*. "Keep away from my stuff."

For a moment I thought she wouldn't move, would just go on rocking gently. Then she said, quite softly, "Make me." Her smile grew wider, became a grin. She whirled and sprinted back down the hallway, holding her arms out from her sides as if she were pretending to fly, brushing her hands against the walls as she ran, laughing. "Make me!" And her bedroom door slammed behind her. I heard her giggling.

I went back upstairs to fix my computer. I was careful about backups, so it wasn't as bad as it might have been. I reloaded all my programs and data and put password protection on. I would make backups even more carefully in the future. It was the best I could do.

I pondered what Lily had said. *They think you're crazy.*

I would need to talk to Vic again. I had to try, even though I knew it would do no good. It would do no good because, about this, Lily had not been lying. They did think I was crazy.

And when I caught myself looking around the apartment for the shadow, listening hard for the humming, hoping, hoping . . . well. I wondered if maybe I was.

CHAPTER 27

Over the next two weeks I became aware that there was something new between Lily and me. I had a peculiar *awareness* of her. For example, when I was in the house—anywhere in the house—I always knew if she was there too; I even knew where she was. Or, if I saw her face, I felt that—if I just tried—I would be able to read her thoughts. I didn't try. These feelings unnerved me horribly. But they were absolutely real. And that this awareness was mutual, that Lily felt it as strongly as I did . . . well, of that I had not the smallest doubt.

It was like that moment just before a summer thunderstorm, when the sky is dark and hot and airless, and you're waiting for the relief of that first explosive clap. But it didn't come.

Perhaps it was this tension that caused Lily to take action. More action. I began to find nasty little surprises in the apartment. Lily, it was clear, had another key.

First, the heap of college catalogs disappeared. On the next day, all the frozen dinners were ripped out of their cardboard containers and thrown into the sink. On the next, the battery was removed from my alarm clock. And after that, incidents mounted rapidly, sometimes more than one a day. Several were merely annoying, like when the glasses and plates switched places in the cabinets, or when the ink cartridge from my printer turned up in my dirty laundry. I actually *expected* the salt in the sugar bowl and the short-sheeted bed. But others were more malevolent: kitchen trash strewn on the floor; the leg of a pair of jeans severed.

They were relatively minor tricks. But cumulatively they upset me even more than the computer incident. Whenever I came back to the apartment, I'd mount the stairs to the attic as if I were approaching a rabid dog. Immediately, I'd search for booby traps; things out of place. Sometimes the Lily-tricks were obvious. But sometimes—like when a rubber band was placed on the spray faucet in the kitchen sink—they weren't obvious at all.

It got so that whenever I was away, at the back of my mind I'd be worrying about what Lily was up to. And when I was in the attic apartment, I'd be tense, wondering what would jump out at me next. By week two, I'd developed a sporadic tic in my left leg.

I knew I ought to do something. But what? Tell Vic? In my head I kept hearing Lily saying, *My parents think you're crazy.* Also, no matter how angry Lily made me, I could not forget that she was only eleven. And that anger was the wrong thing for me to feel. A dangerous thing for me to feel.

I'd been angry at Greg, and Emily had died.

Help Lily, Kathy had said. She was probably right. But she was talking to the wrong guy, in the wrong place, at the wrong time. I couldn't even help myself.

Surely Lily would get bored? Surely this would all go away if I waited?

But one evening I came home to a prank that really hurt, and I boiled over. I pounded down the stairs and barged into the kitchen, where they were all eating dinner.

The smell of Julia's roast chicken was strong, almost overpowering. I stood, a few CDs in my hand. For a long, long moment neither Vic nor Julia seemed even to notice me. Vic absently licked his fingers. Julia cut a green bean in half, her knife clinking decisively on the plate. Lily smiled secretly. I knew *she* knew I was there.

"Vic," I said. "Julia. I have to talk to you."

Julia raised her brows. Vic said, a little uncertainly, "Right now?"

"Yes."

Vic wiped his hands on a paper napkin. "You've been so quiet lately. I was saying to Julia a few days ago that it was almost as if you weren't here . . ."

"I am here," I said. There was a little silence.

"What do you want?" Julia said, pushing her chair back.

I didn't need to look at Lily; I could feel her avid interest. I looked at Vic. I thought of the last time we'd talked. I had believed then that he'd heard me.

I handed Julia the CD cases and she took them reluctantly. Her fingers hesitated over Beck, flinched with distaste at Barenaked Ladies, relaxed in relief on Mozart. She tried to give them back. "I don't understand—"

"Open one of them. Any one. They're all the same, and there's more upstairs."

"David—" Vic began.

I was too aware of Lily. I said rapidly, "None of the CDs will come out. They're glued in their cases. Superglued. Ruined." My voice cracked a little. I steadied it. I looked right at Vic. "Lily did it. I told you, she needs to see a therapist. She's sick. You've got to make her stop doing this stuff."

I expected them to look at Lily then, but they didn't. They looked at me. They kept looking at me. There was no sympathy in their expressions, and I panicked. "Lily did it," I said again. "She ruined my CDs. And she wiped my computer's hard drive, too. And she . . ." I knew it was a mistake. But I couldn't stop myself. I related each of Lily's recent acts of terrorism. With each accusation, I watched for a reaction from Vic and Julia that simply did not come.

At the end I stared, finally, straight at Lily. And she stared right back at me.

She heaved a great sigh. She pushed herself away from the kitchen table, and then at last her parents did turn to her—fondly. She took her plate to the sink. Then she said to her parents, "May I be excused, please?"

"Yes, run along," said Julia and Vic, simultaneously.

Lily edged past me in the doorway and, sheltered from her parents' sight by my body, rapidly and harshly rammed her elbow into my lower back. And with that stab, any hope I'd had of being believed left me.

Lily was too clever for me.

She was right, too. I did look nuts.

We heard the soft sound of Lily's bedroom door closing. Vic stood up. He said cautiously, "Are you mad at Lily, David? Or at us? Because of the girl downstairs, maybe? You don't seem to be seeing her anymore."

I gathered my thoughts. There had to be a way to retrieve the situation. Now that Lily wasn't there, maybe I could make them understand . . . "It's true I haven't been seeing Raina. But this isn't about her, it's about—"

Julia interrupted, but not to speak to me. "Victor," she said to her husband, "we talked about this. I told you my feelings. It should be very clear now that I'm right." Her chin was up. Her mouth was set tight.

"Dear . . ." Vic's voice faltered. Slowly he nodded.

Julia turned to me decisively. "David," she said, "the only way for this to work is for you to simply lead your own life. We must see as little of you as possible." Her voice grew fierce. "And you *must* keep away from Lily. Do you understand what I'm saying?"

The injustice of it took my breath away.

"Do you understand?" Julia insisted.

"Oh, yes," I said. I could not keep the bitterness from my voice. "I understand."

Julia's mouth tightened. "I had my doubts to start with, but I let you come here, because—despite what your mother would say—I am not without family feeling. But now I'm beginning to think . . ." She stopped. She looked at me then like Emily's parents had, when the trial began. With hate.

Hate, not fear. Fear I would almost have understood. Fear was what I felt every day. "Think what, Julia?" I said quietly.

"That you made your own troubles," said Julia. "Like your mother."

I began to turn away then, but she grabbed my arm. "One thing more," she said. "And listen, because I mean it. If you keep it up—if you keep making trouble here—then you will need to leave this house. Immediately. I will not tolerate any nonsense."

I ought to have expected it, but I hadn't. I felt as if the floor had just dissolved beneath my feet. I did not like this house. I had never wanted to be here. And still my stomach lurched as I panicked. What would I do? What would my parents say?

"Now, now, Julia, don't overreact," Vic was saying. He turned to me. "I'm sure that things won't get to that point. Now that we've all talked, and we understand each other."

At that moment my peculiar awareness of Lily kicked in again. She was in her bedroom; I could almost see her. She was seated cross-legged on her bed, and she could hear us perfectly. She was not smiling. She was holding her breath as she waited for my next words.

So when I spoke, I spoke not to them, but to Lily. "If you think that things would go back to the way they were, just because I'm gone, you're wrong. They won't. They never do."

There was a silence. And then Julia said, "I believe

167

that *you*—not Lily—would benefit from consulting a therapist."

I couldn't help it. I didn't mean to do it. But I burst out laughing, and I didn't even really know why. They stared at me. For a few seconds I was truly out of control, and I wondered if I would be able to stop. But then I did.

"Julia," I said, and I wiped my eyes. "If it would help, I'd be on the couch right now. But *my* personal problems"—I looked at Vic then—"have nothing to do with Lily's. Don't you see that? She really does need help."

They kept staring. Implacable.

Finally I shrugged. I turned and went back upstairs, to Kathy's attic apartment.

CHAPTER 28

Still, it itched at me, what Julia had said. Was there some truth in it? Did I make my own troubles? Was I crazy? It seemed—I don't know—it seemed plausible.

After school the next day, I went to the stacks of the public library and found a book on abnormal psychology. I located a list of the behaviors and symptoms often exhibited by those with a less-than-perfect grip on reality.

Stress. I had been under considerable stress for a long time. Stress can put people over the edge, the book stated, using many words of multiple syllables.

Paranoia. I had decided that Lily wanted something from me; maybe hated me; was out to get me; was *capable* of getting me. Was this a sane way to feel about an eleven-year-old girl?

Guilt. I almost laughed. I was qualified to write the Five Books of Guilt.

Visual hallucinations. This was a more reasonable explanation for those sightings of Kathy than believing in the shadow, in the ghost.

Aural hallucinations. The humming. And then in Baltimore, Kathy had talked. Now, if it really was Kathy, why wouldn't she have stayed in Cambridge where she belonged? The answer was obvious: Because she was a hallucination, *my* hallucination. When I moved, she—that is, it—moved also. Not to mention talked.

Clearly, if I was insane, then I was getting worse. The hallucination had changed from a hum to a message. Perhaps it wouldn't be long before the *message* changed—to something less benign. Like, for instance, *Kill Lily.*

I remembered with stunning immediacy the rage that had descended on me the moment I saw Greg punch Emily, just before I threw myself toward him and—

The heavy, thick, hardcover college edition of *Abnormal Psychology* began to slip away from me. I made a two-handed grab for the book and in the process slammed it shut, painfully, on my index finger.

Right then, someone spoke in a muffled whisper from directly beside me. "Yaffe," said Frank Delgado. "Thought that was you." He began to ask me something.

I hadn't even heard him approach. My hands loosened. I turned my head to look at Frank, and he stopped saying whatever it was he was saying. His eyes went from my face down to the book, and he read the title. His eyebrows lifted; he gestured for me to give it

170

to him. I didn't even think of saying no. I flipped it back open and handed it over.

I watched as Frank rapidly read the entire page, and the page before it, and the page after. I watched as he went back and considered the table of contents; the scope of the entire volume. Finally he looked up. "So, who's nuts?" he asked.

"Maybe me," I said. As soon as the words were out I wanted to snatch them back. Time stopped. Frank blurred. The metal-grill floor of the stacks felt wobbly. I could sense the abyss at my feet; the bookshelves seemed, subtly, to shift away. For what felt like forever, I couldn't breathe.

Frank didn't whisper. He said in his normal voice, "Nope."

That was all he said, but I heard him. I heard the certainty in his voice. I saw it in his face too. Air returned to the room. The floor was again solid, and I breathed. I tried to do it quietly. I kept on doing it.

"Let's go," said Frank abruptly. Without waiting for me to agree, he headed out of the stacks. I followed him back into the reference room. He grabbed his coat and books from a table, where mine were also. We left the library.

There'd been something of a thaw the last few days, so it wasn't too cold outside. It was nearly dark, however. We paused at the base of the library steps, facing the park in which the library sat. "Wanna go over to the pizza place?" Frank offered. "Easier to talk with food."

I knew what he meant, but I shook my head. Was I really going to tell Frank what was going on with me?

In the stacks a minute ago I had meant to, but now, outside in the lucid air, I wasn't sure. A big part of me wanted to say, *Just forget it.* "No," I said. "No, I don't want . . ." Abruptly I reversed myself. "I don't want anyone else to hear me."

Frank nodded. "Okay." He settled down on a bench near the big granite slab that said EUCLID. Euclid, the man of logic: two points in a straight line, three points in a plane. I stood uneasily. I waited for Frank to say something. He didn't.

I wandered over to the other slabs. HOMER. VIRGIL. No help there, either. Odysseus and Aeneas were not frightened of eleven-year-old girls.

Frank waited. I wandered back. I said, "Why don't you think I'm nuts?"

"People who're nuts never doubt their own sanity."

"Yeah, the book said that." I didn't look at him. "But I still might qualify. Because I don't really doubt mine." And that was true. No matter what *Abnormal Psychology* said, no matter how many symptoms I exhibited, or what I had done, or what I knew myself capable of, no matter how close, or how wide, the abyss—that was true.

"So somebody else thinks you're crazy?" He sounded entirely matter-of-fact.

I shrugged. "Maybe." I kicked EUCLID. I shoved my hands in my pockets. Then, rapidly, I told Frank the outline. Vic and Julia's marriage problems; that their oldest daughter had died. Lily as go-between. Thanksgiving and the reconciliation. Lily's behavior since; how she seemed to blame me. Raina, and how Lily had spied on us; on her parents. My confrontations with Vic

172

and Julia. That Lily had erased the contents of my computer's hard drive. What Lily had said when I confronted her: *My parents think you're crazy.* The other things Lily had done. My most recent conversation with her parents, and how I had suddenly realized that maybe I *looked* crazy . . . that it *was* possible I was making things up . . . especially if you considered— and this was hard to say aloud, but I did—if you considered who I was. What I'd done.

"You were acquitted," Frank said after an uncomfortable minute. "It was an accident." It was a statement, not a question. I gave him a statement back.

"So what," I said flatly. I looked right at him.

And he nodded. He simply nodded, as if he understood exactly what I was trying to say. And I thought, *Finally.* Finally maybe there was someone I could tell the rest to—about the fear . . .

But then Frank said, awkwardly, "Even that—even how you feel—seems sane to me. I . . . I'd like to think I'd feel the same way if . . . if it were me. And I don't think you're crazy. I believe you. I believe your cousin Lily is the one with a problem."

And with his words I remembered that I needed to talk about Lily. Not about me. About Lily. It took me a minute to get my mind back on track.

"And I also think . . . ," said Frank carefully, when I didn't respond.

"What?" I prompted.

"I think there's something about this situation with Lily that you're not telling me." He paused. "More than one thing?"

Of course he was right. I hadn't told him about

173

Kathy. About the humming shadow. He waited, completely calm, one hand idly tapping his knee. The stubble on his head bristled in the yellow ray of one of the streetlamps. I wondered if hearing would change his mind about my sanity.

"Okay," I said. "It has to do with the oldest daughter. The one who died. I live in her old place, in the attic . . ." I hesitated.

"So what is it?" Frank grinned. "Hey, Mulder. You see her ghost or something?"

I drew in a breath, and let it out slowly. He stopped grinning. He stared at me, and it was only then that I realized he'd been joking. Neither of us spoke for a minute. This time it was Frank, and not me, who broke the silence.

"I'm sorry," he said. "Look, just tell me about it. There must be a rational explanation. I'd guess your cousin Lily is playing more pranks on you, maybe doing something with a flashlight. We'll look at all the evidence and we'll see what comes up. Okay?"

Lily hadn't been in Baltimore when I saw Kathy. Anger gripped me.

"Thank you, Dr. Scully," I said.

He sat up straight. Pointed at me. "Hey, Yaffe, get real. You have a brain. Use it. This isn't some stupid TV show about alien encounters and psychic phenomena—"

"No," I said. "It isn't. This happens to be my life."

"But wait—"

"I gotta go," I said. I don't think I could have gotten a single other word out.

I walked away across the park. Behind me I heard

Frank yell something at me—something like *Go calm down, you moron*. I tuned it right out. He didn't sound angry, but I was. I was choking on rage. Rage and disappointment. I had really thought Frank would listen.

I had even thought, for several minutes, that I could trust Frank with what was really gnawing at me. With the idea that had stolen into my mind a while earlier, without my noticing.

The ghost was nothing. And if Frank couldn't for an instant speculate about Kathy's ghost, then he would not in a million years consider my idea—my hypothesis—my suspicion—my fear that . . . that—

No. It was not an idea, or a hypothesis, or a suspicion. It was knowledge. Conviction.

The things that mattered to Frank—rationality, evidence, proof—I had gone past them. I had made a non-Euclidean leap from point A to point X, and I was on another plane entirely where no one else could come.

No one but Lily.

I was David Bernard Yaffe. I had not meant to kill Emily. I had not meant even to hurt her. But I had, and now I lived forever with the abyss that separated me from people who didn't know what it was like, to have killed. To be a killer.

Acquittal had nothing to do with it. I was a killer. And I knew in my gut when I met another of my kind. Until then, I had refused to see it. I hadn't wanted to know the truth. But the knowledge had been there, somewhere in me, for a long, long time. Guilt knows guilt.

Like knows like.

Lily had killed Kathy.

I didn't know how. I didn't know why. And there was not a chance in the world anyone would believe me. Lily had been seven years old.

Nonetheless, I knew. And, like any textbook-case maniac, like Fox Mulder with his precious files filled with alien encounters, I was utterly convinced of my sanity.

I drove back to the Shaughnessy house, climbed to the attic, nuked a frozen dinner in the microwave, did some homework, and found that Lily had short-sheeted the bed again. I remade it, and then lay in it for several hours. Thinking.

But getting nowhere.

CHAPTER 29

I made it through the rest of that week. Went to school. Said a subdued hello to Raina a couple of times on the front porch. Spent a lot of time aimlessly surfing the Net at the public library. Thoroughly ignored Frank Delgado, who gave up after his third attempt to talk to me. "Fine. Whatever," he said, and walked away.

The guerrilla attacks from Lily continued. I knew she was trying to goad me into a response that would get me kicked out of her parents' house. I was determined not to give it to her. But it was hard. And I also knew that even if I did absolutely nothing, Lily would find some way to make her parents believe I had. It was just a matter of time before they threw me out.

I needed to talk to her.

I didn't want to talk to her.

I was afraid to talk to her.

Partly to calm myself, I bought a chain lock, borrowed Vic's tools from the basement, and installed the chain on the inside of the door to the attic one afternoon when nobody else was around. It would at least ensure that Lily couldn't come up while I was there. But there was no way to keep her out at other times. Not without installing a new lock on the outside, which I didn't dare do.

I tried to work out how Lily might have killed Kathy. How had she made Kathy drink the cleaning solvent? How—

Glass all over the bathroom floor. Lily's knees cut. Lily trying to pull Kathy out. Kathy . . .

Kathy smiling at me, when I was seven and Lily was a newborn.

Emily, so angry at Greg. Emily . . . No! Kathy. Kathy.

One afternoon I took a petty revenge. I had stopped at Tower Records earlier, and when I found that only Lily and I were in the house, I put Talking Heads into the boom box, programmed the track I wanted, and cranked the volume.

Psycho killer, crooned David Byrne. *Qu'est-ce que c'est? Run run run run run run awayyyyyy.* I played it at eardrum-breaking level. It wasn't just revenge. I wanted her to know I knew. I wondered if that would change things, somehow.

My ears rang when I finally turned it off. I put the CD back in its case, and looked around for somewhere to hide it from Lily. In the end I tried shoving it into the back of a tall corner kitchen cupboard, behind a stack of plates. And as I did so, I felt the CD case bump up against something. I reached in and encountered a large, booklike, but oddly soft object. I moved the saucers and pulled the object out. It was a scrapbook.

There was a little dust on the surface. I brushed it off absently, and then opened the book. *Happy 18th Birthday!* said the first page. The words had been written in a glittery gold ink on black paper. I recognized Julia's meticulous handwriting. Beneath the message was glued a photograph of a tiny baby, diapered rump in the air, with a yellow bow somehow affixed to scanty red hair. And under the picture it said: *Kathleen Dawn Shaughnessy: This Is Your Life!*

I took the scrapbook over to the sofa and sat down with it.

There was nothing unusual about the contents. Kathy's baby bracelet from the hospital; infant photos. Then Kathy the toddler: on Santa's lap; cuddling with a younger, glowing Julia; ripping into birthday presents with a little party hat on her head. Kathy a bit older, in front of the house with a plastic shovel, like Lily after her, "helping" Vic clear the walk. I turned the pages and watched Kathy grow up, examined her report cards and school photos. There were some athletic certificates. Lots of pictures of her dancing.

The awkward adolescent phase: pictures of Kathy sullen or wearing too much makeup inexpertly applied, her body too thin in one photo, her face bulging in another. Thirteen, fourteen. A picture of her in her school uniform: short skirt, tight sweater. Defiant eyes. For the first time I saw a faint facial resemblance to

Lily. It made me suddenly aware that there were no pictures of Lily in the scrapbook.

And then, suddenly, a stunningly beautiful girl, blazing out of the center of a slightly out-of-focus photo taken at a party. Kathy was laughing, holding a glass aloft in a toast to the camera, her cheek pressed against that of another girl. *At Rebecca's Sweet 16th,* said the caption. A few other items: ticket stubs from a New Year's Eve Aerosmith concert; a pressed flower from a corsage; a receipt from a clothing store with a shocking total amount on it, circled in red with an exclamation point. Group snapshots with friends: parties, a couple of formal prom photos. An entire page of high-school graduation poses.

Then blank black pages.

I looked up. I half expected to find Kathy's ghost once more sitting beside me. But she wasn't there; I heard no humming, couldn't feel her presence. And, oddly, it was Julia of whom the scrapbook made me most aware. I imagined her collecting all those items carefully, perhaps even rescuing things from the trash. I didn't like Julia; I didn't much want to feel pity for her. But I did.

I wondered what I should do with the scrapbook. Bring it downstairs, leave it there for them? Just give it to Vic and say I'd found it? What would Lily think if I brought them the scrapbook? Would it hurt her? It might hurt all of them; there were still no photos of Kathy downstairs. Part of me liked the thought of hurting them. They had hurt me.

I flipped through the remaining empty pages of the

scrapbook, and found something else. Stuffed between the last page and the back cover was a college blue book, carefully labeled *Anthro 104. Prof. Farris. Midterm exam. Kathleen Shaughnessy.* Idly, I opened it; the first page contained a straightforward attempt to answer an essay question. Kathy had successfully filled one page with vague, rambling comments about adulthood rites in various tribal cultures. But on the second, she faltered. ". . . and I don't care," she'd written in suddenly dark, sprawling print. "What possible difference does it make? You're a jerk, anyway. You should throw out that tie. You're so boring, everyone just dies. Dies dies dies. What if I leave right now? What if I just get right up and walk out in the middle of this test? What would you think of that? What would everyone else think?" And that was all.

I wondered if she actually had walked out of that midterm, if I was looking at the last piece of work she'd done before quitting college. There was no way to tell. Maybe she had finished that particular test. Maybe she'd gotten another blue book, rewritten her essay in it, completed the exam, and turned it in. Slogged on. That was what I would have done. Was doing.

But I knew it wasn't what Kathy had done. I closed the blue book, replaced it in the scrapbook, and tossed the whole thing onto the coffee table. And then I could hear Kathy's voice, once more. Humming, at first. Then, *Help Lily,* it whispered, inevitably. *Help Lily.*

I looked around but didn't see her. Still, the voice continued. And, finally, I answered out loud. "No," I said to the air, to the attic. "I can't. Kathy, don't you see? I have nothing for Lily. I have nothing for anyone. *I can't help.*"

There was silence for only a second or two. Then the humming began again. It had a frenzied quality.

I put my hands over my ears. "No!" I shouted.

Then all the noise did stop.

CHAPTER 30

The next day, I came back to the most alarming Lily-trick yet. Nothing.

At first I couldn't believe it. I did my usual fast circuit of the attic apartment, and couldn't spot anything wrong. Previously this had merely meant that Lily was being subtle. So I did a second and then a third circuit, checking the contents of drawers, all the electrical appliances, and even shaking out the books I'd left lying around. My anxiety increased with every item that Lily had left untouched. I knew something, somewhere, had to be wrong. I remembered the time Lily had put a rubber band on the spray faucet in the kitchen sink—I hadn't discovered that one until I turned on the faucet and got water full in the chest. But at that time I hadn't known how and where to look. I hadn't fully understood how Lily's mind worked.

Still . . . nothing. I stood in the middle of the apartment an hour later, having torn it apart myself in my increasing frustration, and I regarded the chaos. Shelves pulled away from the walls, clothing pulled out of drawers and dumped on the floor, my computer doggedly running redundant loops of virus scans. I could taste the acid panic at the back of my throat.

Nothing.

Lily was downstairs. At that very moment she was lounging on the sofa in the Shaughnessy living room, watching an old movie. I knew she knew I'd ripped the place apart myself, searching for nothing. I knew she knew she'd pushed me almost to the edge.

I knew it.

The bile rose again in my throat and threatened to choke me. In my mind, perfect as a photocopy, I conjured up the page of insanity symptoms from *Abnormal Psychology*. I read them again, and this time . . . this time I thought, *Yeah. Maybe.*

Yes. Finally crazy.

And I found myself sitting on the floor, the floor I'd swept maybe twice in all the months I'd lived there. My chest was heaving, and my breath pumped too quickly in and out of my lungs. And before me, suddenly, I could see Greg and Emily, just as they had been that afternoon, alone in their parents' living room, red-faced, screaming at each other.

> *It was mine, Greg, my money. How could you—*
> *It was mine too. Grandma put the account in both our names—*
> *For school, for my medical school. And now it's all gone—a hundred thousand dollars up your nose—*

184

I don't care, it was mine too—
I won't keep quiet anymore, Greg. I've had it;
you'll pay this time—

Emily didn't even see me; she was crying, crying and screaming and shoving Greg, shoving, and Greg was so much bigger than her, and high and angry and I was afraid he would hurt her, because she wouldn't stop, this was Emily and she wouldn't stop, and he wouldn't either . . .

I just meant to stop it. I just meant to punch Greg.

I could hardly see the attic around me. I had to put my head down between my knees. I tried to breathe slowly and I heard the air wheeze and rattle in my chest. My ears were blocked. I knew too late that I should have gone running; I could have pounded it all out on the pavement. I shouldn't have been there in that cold room, with sweat pouring off me. Remembering was not a good idea. Letting go in any sense was not a good idea.

Did you feel powerful? Did you—

No! I had to deal with the present. With Lily. With Vic and Julia. How could I forget that? How could I lose sight of that?

After a few minutes, somehow I managed to get up off the floor. I held myself upright with one hand on a chair back. I wiped at my face, and my hand came away damp and dirty. My legs steadied. I looked around the room at the havoc I had created.

This could not go on. Lily wanted to play, but I didn't have to. I could deal myself out of the game. I could get some peace and quiet.

185

Why didn't I leave? Why couldn't I just leave?

Wearily, I reached out with my mind for Lily—Lily who I did not need in my life, Lily who would not go away—and I found her. *I'm leaving*, I told her. *I'll find a way to leave, and you can have this place to yourself. If that's what you want, you can have it.*

Lily didn't reply, even though she was there, even though she heard me. She didn't reply.

And then she did. I heard a loud knocking on the downstairs door, immediately followed by Vic's voice. "David? Lily says you want to see us? What's going on?"

"What is it *now*?" said Julia.

I didn't answer. I didn't have the breath for it. I remembered that I hadn't fastened the new chain lock. And so, inevitably, I heard the door open. Determined footsteps came up the stairs. A staccato tread, different from Lily's or Vic's. I had time to wonder if Julia had ever been up to the attic since I'd come. I didn't think so.

Julia stopped dead just inside the doorway, staring at me. First Vic and then Lily came up the stairs in her wake. I heard Vic gasp as he saw me in the middle of the torn-up room. The only other sound was the ticking of the kitchen clock as they stared at me.

I knew what I looked like. I knew what the apartment looked like.

Finally Julia said, "You won't be claiming that Lily is responsible for *this* mess, will you?" Her voice was not unkind. But her glance took in everything I'd done in my mad search for Lily's prank of the day.

Involuntarily my eyes sought Lily. She too was taking in the wreck. Her mouth was ajar. She looked . . . awed.

Yeah, I thought at her sourly. *When I want to be, I'm better at wrecking a place than you are.* Her eyes snapped to mine and for an instant she smiled. Her head made the tiniest of nods.

I said aloud to Julia, "I did this."

I didn't look at Vic because for some reason I couldn't bear to. I didn't look at him even when he spoke. "I'm going to call Eileen."

"No," I said reflexively. "Call my father. I'll give you his pager number, and he'll call back. Don't call my mother."

"But—" I knew Vic had always had trouble talking with my father. So did I. But still, he was the one I wanted.

Julia cut in. "Do it, Victor. Eileen will be no use at all."

I moved slightly then, and Julia flinched. "Don't worry," I told her. I was unable to keep the edge of sarcasm out of my voice. "I'm just going to sit down."

I did that. I sat on the sofa, and told Vic the pager number, and Vic dialed my father. My father called back quickly. I didn't listen to what Vic said to him. It's possible to block things out when you truly need to. Somewhere deep inside I even found room for a little sick humor: At least nobody was telephoning for the men in the white coats to come with a straightjacket.

Yet.

Vic hung up. "Stuart's catching the next shuttle out of National."

"That's that, then," I said aloud. And I looked right

187

at Lily, ready, waiting for her reaction. I said to her, "I'm leaving. It's what you wanted."

I expected her to smile, however covertly. After all, I had conceded completely—and at terrible cost. I couldn't even begin to imagine what would happen to me next. Banishment to Baltimore with the parents that didn't want me? The loony bin? Anything was possible. Lily had more than won. She had destroyed me.

I expected to feel a heavy wave of satisfaction from her. But I stared at her, and she stared back at me, and I could feel what she was feeling, and it was *not* satisfaction. No. It was something quite different. A mix of things. Surprise. Terror. Panic. Fear. I picked them up loud and clear. I kept staring, confused. She didn't want me to leave?

Well, too bad. This was not about her. It was about me. And *I* wanted to leave; I wanted to get as far away from Lily as possible. From Lily, and from Kathy. From every Shaughnessy on every plane of existence.

I shut Lily right out of my head.

CHAPTER 31

Before my father arrived I set the attic to rights again. When I began by shoving a bookcase back against the wall, Julia made a little noise and I thought that she was going to stop me; force me to face my father while surrounded by the chaos I'd produced. With complete clarity I knew I couldn't bear that. But just then Lily got up abruptly and started to help me.

At that moment I'd have taken help from the devil. Lily threw some clothing back in a drawer and pushed it closed, and after that I could almost feel Julia cautiously settle down. Following a few silent minutes of Lily and me working together, Vic too began to sort and fold and pick up and restore.

It didn't take very long to put things back. After all, I hadn't damaged anything. Once we finished, there was an uneasy, waiting feeling in the room. I stood numbly against one wall; Vic and Julia sat side by side; Lily wandered. I supposed, largely uncaring, that Julia and Vic didn't want to leave me alone. No telling what else I might do.

"Do we need to go to the airport to get Stuart?" asked Julia eventually.

Vic shook his head. "He said he'd take a taxi."

"Wasteful," commented Julia. And then suddenly, in a sharply different key: "Lilian! What do you have there?"

Julia's tone penetrated my numbness.

Lily was kneeling on the floor by one of the bookcases, quite near me. She had Kathy's scrapbook in her lap, and she was flipping through the pages rapidly, avidly. At her mother's words, she hunched more closely over the scrapbook, but it was her only reaction. She didn't look up.

"Lilian!" Julia said again as she approached.

Lily's hands tightened on the scrapbook. She had stopped at the page with the picture of Kathy grownup, beautiful, laughing and toasting the camera. Lily stared at it and stared at it. Julia came up beside her and looked down as well, momentarily silent.

"I thought maybe I'd forgotten what she looked like," Lily said finally. It was almost a whisper, and I had the eerie feeling that she wasn't talking to any of us, but to herself.

"Lily . . ." Julia's voice broke. Her eyes met Vic's in a silent plea, and he came over as well. He was a little bit behind Julia in comprehension; he didn't seem to recognize the scrapbook.

"What's that you have?" He reached out. "Lily, can I see what—"

Lily slammed the scrapbook shut and clasped it to her chest. "It's mine!" She glared at Vic, then at Julia. "You can't have it!" She looked a bit demented, face pale and hair mussed, clutching the scrapbook, eyes darting from one parent to the other. "No!" she shouted at Vic, at Julia as they leaned in. "No! Get away!"

"But Lily," said Vic. "What—"

Julia was clearly still incapable of speaking. I said, "It's a scrapbook about Kathy." They all looked at me. "I found it up here. I hadn't had a chance to give it to you yet."

"You looked at it!" Lily snapped, oddly.

"Yes," I said to her. She was very upset; I could almost see the fear and panic pulsing beneath the surface of her skin. Or maybe I thought so only because I could *feel* it, pushing, pushing at the barrier I'd set up in my mind between her and me. "I was curious about Kathy," I said flatly. "I remember her too, you know. Of course I looked." *And I know*, I thought at her. *I know.*

There was a choked little noise from Julia. "We don't speak about her!" she said fiercely to me. "We don't talk about her, we don't . . . don't you . . ." She put one hand briefly to her eyes. She whirled abruptly. Her heels clattered frantically down the wooden staircase.

Vic cast one swift glance at Lily, then at me, and then, making his decision, ran after his wife. "Julia, are you okay? Sweetheart . . ." His footsteps raced into silence.

Alone with me, Lily wrapped her arms even more tightly around the scrapbook, and she rocked slightly with it. Seconds ticked past; a minute. Two. I watched her, and despite myself, despite my numbness, something in me stirred.

My father was on his way. I was in terrible trouble; maybe headed for the psychiatric ward. I had nothing to lose any longer. "Lily," I said, "I know. I know about you."

Lily stilled. Her eyes slitted, ferocious. She said scornfully, "What do you know? You don't know anything!" But I could feel her fear. She couldn't fool me—not anymore.

Maybe, deep inside, she had never wanted to fool me.

I said it gently. "I know you killed Kathy."

My words hung in the attic air like dust.

It felt different saying it aloud to her. The words made it real. And as I watched Lily's face and felt her reaction, I knew for certain—really for certain—that Lily believed it was true.

I wasn't crazy. Or, at least, no crazier than Lily.

I said to her, "Tell me how. Tell me why."

Lily's chest rose and fell. For a moment I actually thought she would burst out with it. But then she caught herself, and the old Lily—distrustful; my enemy—was back, her emotions forced under by sheer willpower. She raised her chin in a Julia-like move. "I'll tell you about me if you tell me about you."

I stared at her. "You already know about me," I said. "Everybody knows."

"But I don't know what you *felt*," Lily said. Whispered. "Tell me what you *felt* after you killed her. And how you feel now. What you feel every day . . ."

Powerful . . . "No," I said, almost before she finished speaking. *No.*

Silence again. Lily bent over the scrapbook, her hair in limp strands over her face so that I couldn't see her expression. Then, softly, she asked, "Why not?" And when I didn't reply, she added, so quietly that it was barely audible, "We're alike, aren't we? You and me?"

If it had been anyone other than Lily, I would have thought she wanted reassurance. Comfort. If it had been anyone other than Lily, I might have found it in me to give those things. But this *was* Lily—Lily who had ruthlessly destroyed what remained of my life, and who might even now be pursuing her own peculiar and particular agenda. I didn't have anything for Lily even if I had wanted to give it.

"Won't you tell me?" she persisted. She looked up at me, her face very pale. "Don't you want to know, David?" She hesitated again. "I'll tell if you will; I really will. And . . . you did ask."

She watched me like a starving mouse.

"You first," I said finally.

She swallowed.

"Go on," I said. "You owe me." And when she still didn't respond, I prompted: "You wanted your sister dead."

Lily's eyes begged me for something, but I didn't know what it was. She looked down. She said, all in a rush, "Everything was always about her. I hated her. Every night, I prayed for her to go away. To die. And then . . . then—it just happened. It was like an experiment . . ." She stopped.

193

I needed to know. I burned to know. I said, "She was taking a bath."

"She knew I was here," said Lily. "She asked me to get her a glass of water."

I have never stood as still in my life as I did at that moment.

"I put some ammonia in the water," said Lily. "I thought she'd smell it. I didn't really think she'd drink it. But she did. She did just exactly what I wanted." Her fist clenched.

Powerful, I thought, watching her, fascinated, horrified. Repelled. Understanding. *Powerful*.

"She had a cold," said Lily. "She had a bad cold. She just . . . she just—" Lily raised her head, and her irises were impossibly huge, liquid with fear and memory. "She just started drinking. I couldn't believe it. I didn't think she really would . . . and then she dropped it. The glass. It broke. It broke all over the floor."

Lily looked at me in wonder, then. "There were so many pieces of glass," she said. "So many."

CHAPTER 32

Acid filled my mouth. I ran for the bathroom, remembered, and diverted to the kitchen sink. I made it only just in time. My forehead, my armpits, exploded with sweat. I emptied my stomach and just kept on retching.

The bathtub. The glass. Lily's knees. My fist. My own fist, aimed at Greg. Aimed at Greg, and hitting Emily.

What was Emily doing there? How had she stepped in the way?

I felt Lily's eyes on me. "Go away," I said. If it hadn't been Emily, would it have been Greg? Would Greg have died, too? Was that what I'd wanted?

"But you promised you'd tell me—"

"Get the hell away from me," I said to Lily. I wasn't watching, but I felt her leave.

Some time after that, my father came. By then I could stand upright. I had just managed to rinse out my mouth and wash my face when I heard the doorbell ring. I heard his voice below. And then—too soon, I was not ready after all—I heard his tread on the stairs. For a moment, I thought my chest would explode.

He stopped in the doorway. We looked at each other.

He was wearing one of his expensive courtroom suits and I wondered fleetingly what he had been doing that day, before receiving Vic's call on his pager. He looked tired.

He came a little farther into the room, closer to me. "David," he said. His arms twitched slightly, as if he'd been about to reach out, but then did not.

I couldn't help it. I practically lunged at him.

I was no longer a child. He wasn't any taller than me. But he closed his arms tightly around me, and said my name again. And I felt then as if I were once more small, and he were a giant. As if in some miraculous way my father could still make everything come right.

Later on he said, "Don't try to talk now. We'll sort it all out later." He picked up the phone and booked a room at a hotel. He packed a few things for me: jeans, sweatpants, T-shirts. He said, "Let's go."

My relief was overwhelming. I didn't care if maybe we were leaving immediately because Vic and Julia had said, *Get him out of our house.* I wanted nothing more than to leave. I walked away from the attic without looking back.

There were a few awkward minutes to endure downstairs. Vic said inane things to which my father variously replied, "I'll be in touch tomorrow. We'll talk tomorrow. I'll call you tomorrow." Julia was nowhere to be seen, which felt fitting. She hadn't been around when I first came to Cambridge, either.

Lily stood apart from Vic. She looked whitened, shrunken. She said nothing to me, nor I to her. For a moment I felt that awareness between us, like a tug on my mind, but then it shut off. *Lily* shut it off. I was glad.

Good-bye, I said silently as we left the house. Good-bye, Vic, good-bye, Julia. Good-bye, Lily. I didn't know what would happen next, but I knew I didn't want to enter that house, or see any Shaughnessy, ever again. Particularly Lily.

I prayed I wouldn't have to.

We're alike, aren't we? she had said. It was true—of course it was true—but I could not live with Lily's intimate knowledge of who and what I had become. Could not bear to look at her and see myself reflected back. Did not want to know that she was there, with me, on the far side of the abyss . . .

Ten minutes later, my father and I checked into the Hyatt Regency on Memorial Drive. Our room was quiet and impersonal; it overlooked the river. I had a long, hot shower. Then I came back out into the bedroom, and looked at my father as he sat on his bed.

"I thought you gave up smoking," I said finally.

He stubbed the cigarette out. "Sorry. I just . . . well, I bought a pack at the airport." He looked at me. He said, "Can you tell me what's going on, David? Why Vic called me—what's going on with you?"

"I want to tell you. But—" I stopped.

"What?"

I said softly, "I'm afraid you won't believe me."

"Why wouldn't I believe you?"

"Because you didn't," I said. "You didn't . . . believe *in* me—before."

He was very still then. "It was just at first . . . I didn't know what to think. And you wouldn't say, you wouldn't talk . . ."

"I know," I said.

He said, desperately, "I love you," and I knew that was true, and I knew it ought to be enough. Especially since—then as before—I still wasn't telling him everything.

I went to the window. I drew aside the curtain and looked down on Memorial Drive and the river. I knew what I wanted. I wanted my father to lie to me. I wanted him to say, *Of course I will always believe you, no matter what.* It was the same thing I had wanted him to say the year before. He hadn't said it then, and he still wasn't saying it. He was promising only what he could promise. He had not changed.

But I had. Somehow, I had.

He said, "Tell me what's happening, David. Please."

I said, "Yes. I'll tell you."

CHAPTER 33

I told him nearly everything. I related all my encounters with Lily, all Lily's pranks. I told him about my conversations with Vic and Julia. What Julia had said about me being crazy; making my own troubles. And, finally, I repeated to him Lily's confession.

The only thing I did not tell him about was Kathy. Kathy, the humming shadow. Kathy, the ghost. I had made that mistake with Frank. I wouldn't make it again.

"Well?" I said into the quiet room, when I was done. "What do you think?" My voice strained a little. "Do you think I made it all up? Like Julia?"

"No," said my father. His voice was strong and sure and thoughtful. "No, I don't think you made it all up. I believe you. Oh, there are a few points on which I'd like more information. Particularly about Lily being responsible for Kathy's death . . . I wonder if Lily has conjured up her own guilt. Children often believe in the power of thought; that wishes can be magical. She certainly *thinks* she killed her sister, but did she? I doubt it. I think she made up a story. But apart from that, yes. Yes, David, I believe you."

He looked straight at me then.

I would have said thank you. I would have said many things, if I could have. I couldn't. Not then. I couldn't speak, even as I heard my father say what I wanted him to say, about talking to Vic and Julia about Lily. I couldn't speak.

Not from relief, although I felt that. Not from gratitude, although that too was strong. Not even because I was afraid I might cry. But because, just then, I heard Kathy whispering once more, in my head. *Lilyhelplilyhelplily.* I stiffened.

I said, to still the voice, "She needs help. Lily, I mean."

"Yes," said my father. "Yes, I think you're probably right. But . . ."

"What?" I said.

"Ultimately, that's up to Vic and Julia." My father pushed his fingers through his hair. "I'll be honest, David. I don't think they're going to listen to me. And I can't *make* them do anything."

I felt as if I were trying to seize hold of air. *Helplily,* came the voice, frantically. *Helplily!*

"I promise to try," said my father. "But you're my first priority. You do see that?"

"Yes," I answered. I sat down on my bed. If my father had not been there I'd have pulled the pillow over my head, squeezed it tightly over my ears. *Helplily.*

My father yawned hugely. "Listen, it's after two in the morning. Let's try to get just a few hours of sleep, okay?" Miraculously, as he spoke, Kathy's whisper faded into silence. My relief was profound.

My father turned off the light. And to my great surprise, with him in the next bed, I slept immediately, and deeply.

I was on my knees by the tub in the attic apartment, vomiting into it. Kathy knelt beside me, the fingers of one hand clawing my arm. She whispered in my ear: *Lilyhelplilyhelplilyhelp*. Around us the air pulsed with intense heat, and the smell of smoke filled my nostrils. Kathy shook me. *Helplilyhelplilyhelp*—

I woke up in the dark. Beside me, my father breathed heavily in sleep. I lay there. And the beat picked up, strengthened, increased in urgency. It pulsed in my ears, then throbbed through my entire body. *Lilyhelplilyhelplily*.

I could not make it stop. And by 3:27 on the digital clock, I couldn't stand it anymore. I had to get away from the pounding.

I padded barefoot to the balcony windows, parted the curtains again, and looked out. The Charles River was iced over and beautiful in the moonlight. Across it I could see the buildings of Boston University, to which I'd applied. Directly in front of me, on Memorial Drive, streetlamps threw regular, dim washes of yellow light onto the pavement. I stared at the lights, at the river, knowing a way to get rid of Kathy's voice, knowing I shouldn't do it. Winter snow and sand had scarred the city streets with potholes. It was purely stupid, dangerous, to go running in the middle of a winter night.

I pulled on sweats despite the thought. I scrawled a quick note in case my father woke up: *Couldn't sleep. Gone running. Back soon.* Then I grabbed socks and my running shoes, and headed down to the ground floor in one of the Hyatt's glass elevators. I couldn't wait to be outside, to race alone through the dark streets, to try to catch up with my own pulse, to drown out Kathy's voice and my own renewed irrational fears.

It was quiet out. Cambridge isn't much of a night town. At first I ran along the river, but it was extremely cold there and I soon headed through the neighborhoods of West Cambridge, running down streets choked with parked cars and snowbanks. The occasional dog barked at me. One even joined me for a mile or so, loping ahead in the dark, then racing back. By the time I hit the Fresh Pond rotary—part of my usual route—I was sweating freely, breathing well. And Kathy's voice had ceased completely.

I felt I could go on forever. I thought about jumping the fence and taking the pretty two-mile route around the pond, but even in my current mood, it was more than I wanted to risk in the dark. Instead, somehow, without any conscious thought, I found myself on Mass. Ave. heading straight north, toward home. No. Not home. The Shaughnessy house. I should have turned around, headed back toward the river and the Hyatt and my father.

I should have turned around.

But I didn't. I *couldn't.* I could not turn back. Instead, as if my body were in thrall to someone else's will, I kept going up Mass. Ave. And my feet were pounding to a rhythm I knew very well. Faster and faster. Faster than I had ever run before. *Lilyhelplilyhelplily.*

I saw the reddening of the sky ahead, and I heard the sirens. And it wasn't just Kathy's will anymore; it was my own. Somewhere deep in my lungs I found a small reservoir of pure oxygenated air, which had been fighting to erupt from my throat in a scream. I forced it down and used it, grimly, to speed up, to race harder, faster. A quarter mile remained; an eighth. A few hundred yards. Another fire truck streaked by me; people spilled out of their houses in bathrobes, slippers, coats. And the whole endless time the scream stayed in my throat, and pounded in my temples, bulged from my eyes.

Crowds of people. I pushed past them frantically, trying to get close to the house, trying to see better against the glare that lit up the sky.

The entire top floor—the attic apartment—was ablaze. The fire must have started there. Below, the air was clogged with smoke. I pushed forward, looking around frantically. Somehow I got to the front of the crowd, to the fire engines, the heavily coated men with their hats and hoses, their ladders. One ladder was just being pulled away from the house. Two firefighters were aiming a hose.

Another got in my way; pushed me back. He snarled something in my face. I ignored him; searched the crowd. "I live here," I snarled back at him. I called, "Vic! Julia! Raina!" I yelled, "Lily!"

I screamed, *"Lily!"*

Ahead of me I saw Julia, draped in a man's coat. Her

cheekbones jutted out against the red sky, her gray hair frizzed around her head. She was staring at the house, shaking, her arms clasped about her. She moved, and I saw that Vic was beside her. I even saw Raina, a little distance away. She had two canvases with her, held upright by her arm.

"Where's Lily?" I shouted at the firefighter. "Where's the little girl?"

"She's around here somewhere," he answered. "Now, get back! It's dangerous here!"

Kathy had gone. The pulse in my head was gone. I stared at the fire, terrified. Because I *knew* the firefighter was wrong. Lily was still in the house. The burning house.

I knew exactly where Lily was, and what she was doing, and even why. I also understood, finally, why I had come there, and what I must do. *Help Lily.*

I shouted aloud to Kathy above the roar of the fire: "Yes. I will."

CHAPTER 34

I sprinted for the house. I heard somebody shout, felt a grab at me that failed. Behind me as I reached the front porch, I heard more yells, but I knew no one could stop me, no one would pursue me—not even the firefighters. It was too dangerous. I pounded up the stairs to the second-floor landing, into Julia and Vic's apartment.

The heat hit me like a brick wall. I gasped, and nearly choked on smoke. I grabbed the hem of my sweatshirt and pulled it up over my nose and mouth. It reeked of sweat. I raced down the hall and through the living room, and nearly crashed into the door to the third-floor apartment. Behind my hand, behind the door, I could feel even more intense heat. I could hear the crackle of flames.

My heart felt like it would jump from my chest. My lungs ached. I pulled at the knob. The door was unlocked, but Lily had secured it on the inside—with the chain I had so recently, so carefully, installed. I thought wildly about running at the door and shouldering it down. But the hinges were on my side; it wouldn't have worked.

There were only two hinges. I reached for the top one and snatched my hand back. Painted metal. Hot.

I pulled my sweatshirt completely off and used it to protect my fingers as I unscrewed the top hinge from its casing. Thank God Vic took good care of the house; the hinge was well oiled and unfastened easily.

I didn't bother to unscrew the lower hinge; I grabbed the higher one and pulled, until the door parted from the frame and I could get my fingers around the door itself. Then I brought my weight down, down against the bottom hinge.

The hinge ripped away from the frame. The door crashed open. I ducked out of the way. Heat descended in a rush from above; a fierce roar pounded at me.

Before me was the old steep wooden staircase. Smoke roiled down the passage and enveloped me. I coughed. I shoved the sweatshirt over my face again and breathed in the stink of my own sweat and fear. I knew this place; I didn't need to see. I ran up, directly into the smoke and haze. The snap of the fire filled my ears.

I reached the attic. I pulled the shirt away from my eyes.

The walls and the windows at the front and back of the apartment were thoroughly engulfed; the roof was half gone, open to the night. But the side of the attic was still whole, though the flames were eating their way across the floor.

206

Still holding my shirt over my mouth, I made my way to the bathroom. And there I found Lily exactly where I knew she'd be—lying down in the tub, faceup, immersed in water.

Only her nose was above the water line. She was holding herself entirely rigid, but her chest lifted with her breath. She was alive. She was waiting. For Kathy? For me?

Her head lifted and her eyes flew open. She raised her head farther out of the water and began to scream.

"Get out! Get away! Leave me alone!"

I fell to my knees and hauled her out of the water and into my arms. It was like the torture-museum dream. I could barely breathe. My eyes smarted from the smoke. The skin of my bare back felt as if it was melting. For an instant I put my face against Lily's wet neck and breathed. I put my mouth up close to her ear.

"I'm taking you out of here!" I yelled.

"No! No! No!" She flailed frantically, trying to scramble back into the tub.

Lily was strong, but I was stronger and more desperate. We had very little time before the flames consumed that ancient staircase. With one hand I grabbed a big bath towel from the rack behind me and soaked it in the tub. Somehow I got it around my shoulders, around Lily. It was a good thing she was already wet. She yelled again and squirmed. "Shut up," I told her. "Shut up and be still!"

She kicked viciously. I got up anyway, and staggered back into the living room.

In the few minutes I'd been with Lily in the bathroom, the fire had spread. It had formed a sheet of

207

flame over the entire front of the living room. The sheet had just reached, and covered, the open doorway to the stairs down. I couldn't see past it. The stairs—our only escape route—were surely only seconds from going up in flames.

In my arms I felt Lily turn. She saw the sheet of flame before us, and for an instant she stilled. Whimpered. Her arms tightened around me. "I have to die," she said urgently. "I killed Kathy. And I meant to do it. I'm a murderer."

"I know," I said. For a bare instant our eyes met, hers now wide with astonishment and—something else. Something I didn't have time for. "But your punishment isn't to die. It's to live with it. Like me, Lily."

Like me.

She gasped. "Hold on," I said. I pulled the wet towel completely over her head. I'd lost my sweatshirt somewhere. I buried my own face in the towel for an instant and took a deep breath. Then, holding Lily tightly, I ran directly into the sheet of flame that blocked the stairs.

In the middle of fire, time changes; elongates, shortens. Pain is everywhere and nowhere, but there is no room for fear. Whoever conceived of hell as fire understood its nature.

But also didn't.

We passed through the fire, Lily and I. It took less than a second; it took forever. Then we were on the staircase that—God be praised—was not yet fully consumed. I felt one of the boards crumple beneath my foot, but our combined weight had already shifted on and down. Down.

Down.

I have no memory of running through the Shaughnessy living room, or the hall. I do not recall the other staircase, the one that took us safely to the ground and out of the building just as the entire third floor, and part of the second, collapsed behind us. I do not remember stumbling on the porch and tripping down the stoop onto the small front lawn. I never saw the firefighters, though I'm told they were ready for us with a fire blanket that they threw over my head and back—an act that probably saved my life, since my hair and back were aflame. I do not recall that first surge of breathable air in my lungs. I have no memory of throwing myself on the earth, of rolling, rolling blindly in that blanket, still holding Lily, still clutching Lily, still protecting Lily.

I remember only one thing. I remember that from the moment I pronounced her punishment and joined it with mine, Lily held me. She held me as we passed through that sheet of flame. She held me through that nightmare run through the house. She held me in the frozen winter air, as the Cambridge fire department extinguished what remained of the fire that had tried to destroy us. Through all of it, Lily held me, and I held Lily. Together, we survived.

We lived.

CHAPTER 35

"**F**ace it," I said with careful nonchalance to my parents from my hospital bed. It was three days later; I lay on my stomach in a private room while a lovely intravenous needle channeled painkillers through my system. "Fate never intended me to complete high school. Can't I just take the equivalency test?"

Frank Delgado laughed. He was pacing idly back and forth at the foot of my bed, his presence making the room feel even smaller. I was glad he was there.

"No, you can't," said my mother, with a swift reproachful glance at Frank. Frank had shown up the day before, slipping past the security guard my father had hired to keep the reporters out.

I wanted to see Lily—desperately I wanted to see Lily—but that hadn't yet been permitted. I was biding my time. I hoped she knew I was thinking about her. I thought she did.

She was in the hospital too. Although she had not been physically harmed, there was no concealing the fact that she had set the fire, that she had run back in after seeing her parents and Raina to safety. She was classifiable now: a fire-setter. Suicidal. She was where I had always thought she should be: in the hands of trained psychiatrists.

At one time I'd have felt good about that, but I was no longer sure. I needed to see her. Talk to her.

But I had to wait.

My father was saying, "I've already arranged with Dr. Walpole for tutors. They'll bridge the next month, and then the doctors say you'll probably be ready to go back to St. Joan's."

Oh, really? I thought, diverted momentarily from thinking of Lily. *And just where am I going to live?* In the Hyatt where Vic and Julia were now staying? I doubted it. They had come by exactly once, thanked me stiffly and insincerely, and left.

I knew they blamed me for the loss of their house, their illusions, and—in a way—their second daughter. I knew they would not forgive me, ever.

A small hard voice in me said that I didn't forgive them, either.

My father's words penetrated. "We're still working on living arrangements for you, David, but we have something in mind. We need a couple more days."

I stiffened, and then controlled myself. I didn't want a fight. But the thought of another parent-conceived living arrangement made me feel distinctly queasy.

"There's a spare room at my house," said Frank idly. "My mom would be okay with it."

I blinked, interested. I raised an eyebrow at my father, but my mother was looking at Frank in ill-concealed dismay. "Thank you," she said hastily. "But as my husband says, we're working on something else."

My mother was unsure about Frank. In particular, she didn't care for his solution to my hairstyling problem. I had let Frank loose with scissors and an electric razor that day. My parents had arrived later to find me just as bald as he was.

"It will all grow back, won't it?" my mother had asked urgently, unnecessarily. After all, my scalp had not burned, only my hair. It was my back that would need a skin graft.

"But it's not so bad, on the whole," the specialist had said, changing the dressing. "You were very lucky, young man."

I was lucky in another way, too. Nearly all the reporters had finally given up; moved on to other, more important, stories. But the day after the fire, there had been cover stories in all the local papers. The stories, my father told me, had featured still photos taken from a video that a neighbor shot. The video itself had made both the local and national news. I had seen none of it, and I didn't want to. I'd heard enough from the nurses, the doctors. Everybody seemed to think I was a hero. It was more pleasant than the previous year's tide of hate, but just as wrongheaded, just as misinformed.

I closed my eyes just for a moment. My mother noticed and leapt to rush everybody out of the room. I needed peace, she said. I needed to rest. They'd be back later.

I was tired. But even so I didn't much like being alone. I couldn't stop thinking, worrying, about Lily. I didn't want to. We weren't finished, Lily and I.

I wondered what Kathy would think about what had happened. I wondered if this was the kind of help for Lily she'd had in mind. I wondered what the psychiatrists would make of Lily, and she of them. I wondered and I worried.

The next morning I asked once more to see Lily, and once more my parents exchanged glances, and told me I would have to wait. I said then, bluntly, "Has Lily asked to see *me*?"

"Yes," said my father after a moment.

"What's the problem, then? Is it Julia? Vic?"

My father sighed. "You have to give Julia time, David."

"I'm not interested in Julia!" I snapped. "Or Vic. I'm interested in Lily. Don't you see—"

"It's not our decision," my mother said. "It's Vic and Julia's. Please understand, David, there's nothing we can do."

"I saved Lily's life—"

"There's nothing we can do." They said it together, almost in sync, and then glanced at each other, embarrassed.

I shut up. But I brooded. And later that afternoon, I talked to Frank. I had to talk to someone, or burst.

"So you just want to speak with her?" he said at the end.

"Yeah. I know it would help her. I just know." I paused. "And it would help me, too. It's just . . . it's important."

Frank leaned forward in his chair, steepling his hands. "What if I could sneak in to her?" he said. "With a message?"

I stared at him. My mind whirred. I imagined there'd be tight security on the psychiatric ward—but Frank had, after all, gotten past my father's hired guard.

"What do you have in mind?" I asked.

"I'll think of something. Trust me." He shrugged. "What's the worst they can do? Throw me out? I'm out already." He was utterly calm. I thought how much I liked him.

"Well?" said Frank. "Should we do it?"

"Yes," I said.

He was intent. "Okay. I'll try tonight. What should I tell her if I get in?"

"Tell her . . . say . . ." I paused to gather my thoughts.

On the night I told my father about Lily, he had given me the reaction of a reasonable, logical person. I knew the psychiatrists would be the same. Lily would have told them she was responsible for Kathy's death. But who would believe that a seven-year-old girl could actually commit murder? Far easier, far more sensible, to think that she had imagined it out of guilt and fear. Yes, the psychiatrists would tell Lily that she had made up a story.

The point was . . . the point was it didn't matter. To Lily it was one and the same. She needed to be believed.

I *did* believe her. Possibly no one else ever would.

"Tell Lily," I said to Frank, "that I believe her."

"That's it?" said Frank.

214

"Yes." I hesitated. "Frank?"

"Yeah?"

"Thank you," I said.

He ducked his head. Its bald pate gleamed under the fluorescent lights. "It'll be fun." He paused, and then said, "One more thing." He reached into his backpack, pulled out a manila envelope, and tossed it on my bed. "This is for you," he said, and left.

Something from school, from Dr. Walpole? I opened the envelope, and pulled out a small drawing in charcoal and red ink. Caught my breath. I recognized the artist immediately: Raina. And the subject: my face.

The drawing blurred before my eyes. I had a sudden vivid memory of her other drawing of me; the one I'd destroyed. I could see the mouth in that one, as it gasped for breath at the bottom of the dish of water.

I couldn't stand to look closely at this one. Not right away. I shoved it back into the envelope and threw it into my bedside drawer. I wondered if Raina had found Frank, or he her. I wondered if I wanted to see Raina. I thought so.

But not yet.

I waited up all night for Frank, but he didn't come and he didn't call, and I had no message from Lily.

CHAPTER 36

The next morning, my parents bounced in. My mother was glowing. "We signed the sublease." She smiled warmly at me. "It's a wonderful place, David—three bedrooms, furnished, overlooks the Charles. It belongs to a couple of professors on sabbatical. You can walk to school. I can't wait!"

I stared at her. "What?"

"We're moving up here for the rest of the year," said my father calmly. "Your mother got six months' leave of absence from the library. I had most of my cases reassigned, though I'll still keep my eye on a few from up here. And I'll need to fly back down to D.C. for a few court dates."

"I'm going to take some courses at Harvard Extension," announced my mother. "I've got my eye on one—"

"Wait," I said to my parents. I needed to make sure I understood. "You're moving up here to . . ."

"To be with you," said my mother. "While you finish out the school year. Isn't it exciting? We'll be a family again." Her voice faltered then. "David?"

I felt . . . I didn't know what I felt. For the flicker of an instant it was August again, and I was alone, sweatily trudging upstairs to the Shaughnessy attic with armloads of stuff. I could almost see the attic apartment, Lily seated on the floor in its very center. *I should live here*, she had said then. Instead—perhaps because of me—she had selected it to die in.

They were looking at me, and my father was wearing one of his courtroom faces: still, watchful. I looked back. Did my parents think we could simply erase the past few months? That, here in another city, we could be who we'd been before? That, magically, I would again be the Davey they'd once loved?

There was still Emily. There was always Emily.

My silence had gone on too long. My mother turned abruptly and left the room. My father walked to the window so that I had an excellent view of his back. He said then, "I suppose we should have asked you first."

"Yes," I managed finally.

"I—" He stopped. "I take it then that you don't think this is a good idea."

I cleared my throat. "I don't know . . ." I couldn't go on.

"We could cancel the lease," said my father's back. "You could live with Frank, if that's what you want."

217

"Give me a minute!" I burst out. "Can you please just give me a minute!"

He did. The minute elongated. I blinked hard. I tried to gather my thoughts.

As if my silence were puppet strings pulling on him, my father turned. His hands dangled. His shoulders were braced.

In a way it was like looking at that sheet of fire before I ran through it with Lily. I had come to Cambridge on my parents' assurance that it was the right thing to do. I *had* to say what I thought. What was true. Even if it hurt them. Even if it hurt me.

"If we're a family again," I said slowly, "you have to understand . . . it won't—it can't—be like before. I'm not the David you used to know."

I was silent for even longer then, and he let me be. Finally I found words. "I killed my girlfriend, my lover," I said to my father. "I live with that now. I will always live with it. I choose to live with it, because otherwise—otherwise I would have to die."

Lily had taught me that truth. Her truth. And I would now try to teach her mine. *Your punishment is to live with it.*

Perhaps shared, the burden would grow easier. Perhaps, up ahead, I'd find ways to atone. Strangely, I had hope for that now. Somehow, Lily—saving Lily—had given me hope. Lily needed me. And I needed her.

To heal. If we could.

What my father needed to understand, however, was that there was no going back. That I no longer had the guarantees of a regular, "normal" future. That I didn't even want them. Not anymore.

I looked at him now, straight on. My father's eyes held guarded nightmares. They were the eyes from the famous photograph. He said heavily, "I know that's how you feel. But I don't want it to be that way for you."

"I know," I said to him. "You and Mom both. But please see. *For it to be any other way—for me—would be wrong.*"

He held my eyes. He was silent.

I said, "I am someone different from the son you planned and hoped for. I don't know yet who that is." And then I was the one who had to look away. I swallowed. "I can't change Emily's death. But there will be things—I hope there will be things—that you can be proud of. One day. They just . . . they won't be the ones you wanted. Before."

I said the last thing then. It was a gift to him. I had said it under oath, but never had I said it directly to my father. Even though I knew he needed to hear it.

I said: "Dad. Before. I never hit Emily. I never laid a hand on her that wasn't—" I stopped and then continued. "—that wasn't in love. I swear to you. I swear it."

He put his hands on my shoulders, and I winced as the burns flared with new pain. My father snatched his hands away as if they too were on fire. "Why didn't you tell me before?" he asked. "Why did you only say it on the stand—only when you had to?"

I said, "I wanted you to know without asking."

We looked at each other.

"I'm sorry," said my father. He sounded exhausted. "I'm not . . . I'm not built like that."

I nodded. He was a criminal lawyer. Somewhere in

me I knew that I was still disappointed, would always be disappointed. But it was time to let that go. "No," I said. "I'm the one who's sorry. I was being a child."

"You are my child," said my father.

We were quiet.

"Why did Greg lie?" asked my father, finally. I flinched, even though I knew it was not because he doubted me. It was because he wanted every thread tied.

"I don't know for sure," I said. "I have guesses, but I will never know." I looked at him then. "I loved *him* once, too," I said, with difficulty. "He was my best friend. That last year, he really was doing a lot of coke. I was occupied with Emily; I wasn't paying much attention to him. I don't know if . . ." I stopped. "I don't know," I said again, more strongly. "By the end, I didn't know Greg. I didn't know him at all."

There was silence. I waited until my father chose to speak—and had a glimpse, then, of how it had been for him, waiting for me. But after a minute or two he said, quietly, "I *am* proud of you, David. Not someday. I'm proud of you right now."

He swallowed audibly. "When I woke up the other night at the Hyatt, and you weren't there . . . when I saw your note . . . and then the phone rang, and it was the police . . . when I got to the hospital . . . and Julia, Vic . . ." His voice broke completely, and I realized I hadn't thought to ask for the story of the night of the fire from his point of view.

"I have that video," my father went on. "I've watched it a dozen times. And every time I think how you almost died. I wasn't there; I didn't help; we put

220

you there, in danger. I didn't understand what you told me about Lily. I can't . . . I can't . . . "

He sat down in the chair that my mother had vacated. He held his face in his hands. His shoulders heaved. And then he looked right up at me, and he said clearly, "They had to sedate Lily to get her away from you that night. After you fainted; when you were in the ambulance. I wish I could arrange for you to see her. There's nothing I . . ."

I stared at him.

"You're right," said my father. "You're not . . . you're no longer who you were. And you're not the son I thought you were going to be. But I don't care. I barely remember who that was. That boy—that man— wasn't real. You are.

"I couldn't be prouder," said my father. "David. I simply couldn't be."

My father took off his glasses, wiped them clean, and put them back on. He began to wander the room. "I was looking forward to living here for a while. I haven't since law school, you know. And your mother wants to take a course at Harvard Extension: 'Deciphering Ancient Maya Hieroglyphs.' "

At last I knew what I felt. Warm. Like I'd been propped on pillows and wrapped in a blanket. "I wouldn't want her to miss that," I said. "Uh . . . did you want to take it too?"

"No, something else caught my eye," said my father.

"What?"

"Beginning saxophone." We looked at each other and I knew that, at least for the moment, I understood him and he understood me. Maybe one day I'd think it was worth what had happened to me to get to this place.

It would never be worth Emily's death.

I found my voice. "Welcome to Cambridge, Dad."

My father's face went very still. "We should have come in August," he said. "With you."

I said, "I don't know. But I'm glad—"

"Yes," said my father. And then, after another whole minute, he went off to find my mother.

CHAPTER 37

I awoke suddenly. There was a flashlight shining directly into my face. Then it snapped off and a voice grunted, "It's Frank."

"What took you—"

His hand clamped down over my mouth. "Shhh! This place is packed with professional paranoids who think everything is their business."

My bedside clock said 2:05. Careful of my back, I eased myself up to sit on the edge of the bed. Frank had cupped the flashlight in his palm so that there was only the faintest light inside the room, but more filtered in from around the edges of the door, which he had left slightly ajar. Next to him in the dimness there was a wheelchair, and in that wheelchair . . .

"Lily," I whispered. I didn't think; I opened my arms. There was a squeak from the wheels as Lily hurtled out of the chair and landed against me, hard. Her hands scrabbled directly on top of the dressings. It hurt horribly and I barely noticed. "Hey," I said. She was shaking but not crying. Not my Lily. I held her with one arm and stroked her hair with the other. Even in the fire, she had not held me so fiercely. "Hey," I said. "I'm here."

Her voice was muffled. "Don't go away."

"I won't," I said, and I thought of Boston University, just across the river.

We were quiet then, my cousin and I, in the almost-dark.

After a bit I looked over Lily's head toward Frank. He was peering out into the corridor. "All the other patient doors are wide open," he said matter-of-factly. "Eventually someone's going to want to look in here. Plus, I think we've got about fifteen minutes before I have to get Lily back up to her bed. I'm taking advantage of a shift change upstairs."

In the stronger light by the door, I could see that Frank was wearing a green smock with a badge on it. And—

"What's that on your head?" I asked. "A squirrel?"

"I think I'm very attractive as a blond. The woman in personnel hired me this morning." Frank's teeth gleamed. "I'm an orderly. They were desperate. Nobody wants to work the night shift."

An amazing guy, Frank. "Thanks," I said, inadequately. "Thanks."

He nodded. "I'll be back in fifteen." He slipped out into the hospital corridor.

In my arms I could feel Lily's weight. Fifteen minutes.

"I asked for you," Lily whispered.

"I asked for you." I paused. "What have you told them?"

She sighed, and I felt it against my skin. "It's bad, isn't it?" I said.

"They don't believe me. About Kathy. You know."

I knew. I hugged her, but at that moment it wasn't the right thing to do and she stiffened. I loosened my arms and she settled down, but I could feel the caution in her. This was still Lily.

She said, as she had in the attic, "David, please tell me—how do you *feel*? Now? Every day?"

I drew in a breath. And then I told her, articulating it aloud for the very first time. "I think of it as an abyss. Before, you're standing on one side of it, with everyone else—and you don't even see it. And then, after, you're on the other side.

"And it doesn't matter," I said with difficulty. "It doesn't matter how you got there, or whether you never *meant* to do anything so horrible. What's true every day is that you are on the other side. Alone. Knowing—"

"That you could do it again," finished Lily softly. "That it's possible."

Anyone in this world can have the power of life and death over someone else. It's horrible, but true. All you need do is take it. And once you have—there is no going back.

"Yes," I said to Lily. "It's always possible now. For us."

We were silent. Then Lily said starkly. "How can I be sure I won't do it again someday? Now that I know I *can*?"

225

We can't be sure, I thought. *Nothing is sure. But . . .*

I said, "Do you want to do it again?"

"No!" said Lily. "No!" I heard the raw truth in her voice. "I think about *her*—about my sister—every day. But still, sometime I *might* . . . even just for a second . . . and what if . . . what if . . ."

What if.

I said, "I'll make you a deal, Lily."

She waited, tense.

"We'll help each other," I said. "When it hurts, when we're afraid, if we're ever tempted—we tell each other. I'll help you. You'll help me. We won't use the power we have. And we'll find ways to do good. To . . . to atone."

Quiet, as Lily thought about it. I discovered I was holding my breath.

I said, "Is it a deal, Lily?"

And Lily said, like a vow: "Yes."

"That's that, then," I said.

We held each other in the dark for the time we had left.

After Frank took Lily away, I turned on my light. I reached into the bedside table and pulled out the envelope that Frank had brought. I took out Raina's drawing and unfolded it steadily. I looked.

Just a face. An ordinary one, really. The lips didn't smile, but they were calm. The chin was a mere line, firmly, swiftly done: unmistakably mine.

And yes, there was something nameless in the eyes; something you didn't want to see or acknowledge. But you knew, looking, that the owner of those eyes was

226

not flinching. That he called his demons by name, and kept them at bay. And always—somehow—would.

I took in a deep breath. Then I looked even more closely at the eyes, at the tiny figure Raina had placed in each iris. In the left: a woman. In the right: a little girl.

They were not demons, the woman and the girl. They wore tiny wings.

EPILOGUE

On my first night in the new apartment with my parents, I dreamed I stood in the Porter Square Star Market, in the "8 items or less" checkout line. In front of me in line stood a redheaded woman. She turned. It was Kathy.

She didn't seem surprised to see me. She fumbled inside a tote bag and pulled out a supermarket card. Gravely, she offered it to me. I pulled out my own.

Silently we swapped, and I examined my new card. It said DAVID YAFFE. I looked up and met her eyes. She held out the card I had just given her, so that I could read the name on it.

It said LILY SHAUGHNESSEY.

She smiled, and so did I. One way or another, people always do smile in Cambridge when they trade supermarket cards. Kathy's smile was not the usual one, however. It was simply radiant. It warmed me all the way to my soul. Then she ducked her head and turned away. And I woke up, compelled by an urgent impulse.

It was just dawn. Still awkward, I got out of bed and went over to the bureau. I opened my wallet and pulled out my Star Market card.

It said DAVID YAFFE.

ACKNOWLEDGMENTS

I'd like to thank the many people who helped me during the years I worked on this book. Elaine Werlin, Arnold Werlin, Max Romotsky, Miriam W. Rosenblatt, and Susan Werlin: for loving and believing in me. Jayne Yaffe: for loaning her family name. Discerning early-and-often readers Victoria Lord, Ellis O'Donnell, and Barbara Hillers. My online writers' group, for always being there. Dian Curtis Regan, Jane Kurtz, Jo Stanbridge, Debbie Wiles, Franny Billingsley, Toni Buzzeo, Walter Mayes, Amy Conklin, Conrad O'Donnell, Anneke Kierstead, Jan Smith, Sharyn November, Athena Lord, and Jackie Briggs Martin: for various critical and informational help and encouragement over time. My agent, Shelley Roth, for her straightforwardness and meticulousness.

Most importantly, I owe thanks to my editor, Laura Hornik, for her belief in David's story, and for kindly but firmly pushing me to tell it as well as I possibly could. There may be other editors who are more intelligent, creative, thoughtful, and critically acute—but I can't imagine how.

LOCKED INSIDE

At sixteen years of age, Marnie Skyedottir had a personal net worth of $235.27 million. That she made do on $50 a week was the work of Marnie's guardian, Max Tomlinson, and Marnie knew that one day—on her twenty-first birthday, to be exact—she could, if she chose, have revenge.

"I'll fire your sanctimonious butt, Max," she told her computer screen, where a characteristically lengthy and courteous e-mail from Max lay open. (. . . *As you know, the regulations for Halsett Academy for Girls clearly stipulate that students on academic probation should not have access to excess personal funds. . . .*) Marnie could almost hear Max speaking the words in his Mississippi lawyer's drawl that, for all its leisured pace, somehow never sounded any less than definite.

"Your years managing my life will be over"—she

jabbed at the keyboard with satisfaction and precision—"like that."

Max's e-mail disappeared into the Trash. Marnie blinked and only then realized her eyes hurt. Burned. And her shoulders ached. She flexed them, and shut her eyelids tightly for a few seconds. Well, no wonder she was in pain. Before the reply from Max had arrived, she'd been online for a while, chasing that clever, thieving, infuriating Elf through the dark winding virtual alleys of Upper Paliopolis. She glanced down at the clock on her computer. 5:43 A.M. Max was up early in New York City, in that huge duplex apartment on Central Park West that Marnie was supposed to call home. Ha.

Wait. 5:43 A.M.?

"No!" Marnie moaned instinctively, and then clapped a hand over her mouth. Dorm walls weren't very thick. But it couldn't be. She couldn't have been online for over ten hours! She directed a fierce glare at the clock, as if she could will it to spin backward to, say, 10 P.M. Early enough for her to go over her chem notes and then go to bed at midnight, like a good preppy Halsett girl—like Jenna Lowry or Tarasyn Pearce or someone like that.

Instead the clock went forward. 5:44 A.M. And her computer beeped as words appeared in the Paliopolis chat window. A message from that pesky Elf glowed neon in the dark of Marnie's room.

Giving up? The sneer was implicit.

Marnie hesitated. She disliked her chemistry class with its brooding, angry teacher, and she wasn't doing well in it. There was no chance of sleep now, but if she at least spent an hour with the notes, maybe she could pass the test today.

Thanks for the spellbook, Sorceress, the Elf gibed. *You'll be a lot more helpless without it. I'm looking forward to watching your rating plummet. While mine soars!* The message was accompanied by a belching raspberry noise; Paliopolis sound effects were crude but effective.

Well, who needed sleep? The Elf had been on just as long as Marnie, and if he could keep going, so could she. Or rather, so could her alter ego, the Sorceress Llewellyne. It was not for nothing that Llewellyne had the highest player rating in all of Paliopolis.

Marnie grinned and attacked the keyboard. *Dream on, you drooling nitwit,* she typed to the Elf.

She had more than two hours before she had to be in class, anyway.

Another compulsively readable thriller
from Nancy Werlin

THE RULES OF SURVIVAL

A NATIONAL BOOK AWARD FINALIST
AN *LA TIMES* BOOK PRIZE FINALIST

★ "Brilliant." —*Booklist*, starred review

"One of literature's most despicable mothers." —*Publishers Weekly*

★ "Heartbreaking." —*Kirkus Reviews*, starred review

★ "Teens will empathize with these siblings and the secrets they keep in this psychological horror story." —*SLJ*, starred review